P9-ARH-222

WITHDRAWN

THIS IS THE WAY THE WORLD ENDS

ALSO BY JEN WILDE

Going Off Script

The Brightsiders

Queens of Geek

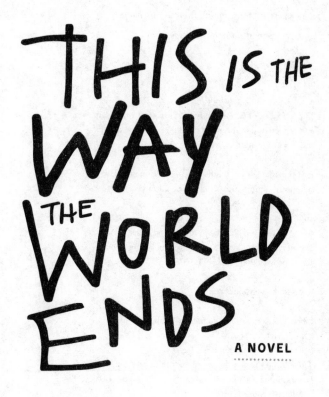

THIS IS THE WAY THE WORLD ENDS

A NOVEL

JEN WILDE

WEDNESDAY BOOKS
NEW YORK

To my cats,
who never left my side as I wrote this book,
and yet were of no help whatsoever

. . . .

First published in the United States by Wednesday Books,
an imprint of St. Martin's Publishing Group

www.wednesdaybooks.com

Library of Congress Cataloging-in-Publication Data

Names: Wilde, Jen, author.
Title: This is the way the world ends : a novel / Jen Wilde.
Description: First edition. | New York : Wednesday Books, 2023. |
    Audience: Ages 12–18.
Identifiers: LCCN 2022056026 | ISBN 9781250827975 (hardcover) |
    ISBN 9781250827982 (ebook)
Subjects: LCGFT: Novels.
Classification: LCC PZ7.1.W533 Th 2023 | DDC [Fic]—dc23
LC record available at https://lccn.loc.gov/2022056026

Our books may be purchased in bulk for promotional, educational,
or business use. Please contact your local bookseller or the Macmillan Corporate
and Premium Sales Department at 1-800-221-7945, extension 5442,
or by email at MacmillanSpecialMarkets@macmillan.com.

First Edition: 2023

10 9 8 7 6 5 4 3 2 1

Do not go gentle into that good night.

—DYLAN THOMAS

CHAPTER ONE

We really should be studying," I call from inside Caroline's massive walk-in closet. It's almost as big as my whole apartment. A tall window looks out over Central Park, the buildings on the other side silhouetted by the setting sun. Pinks fade into orange and purple in the sky; lights flicker on in apartment windows, the treetops below soaking up the last of the golden-hour rays. I turn to the floor-to-ceiling collection of shoes, running my fingers over suede heels, then velvet boots, then studded sneakers. A marble mood board covers the opposite wall, a collage of prom dresses, cute summer outfits, and models like Cara Delevingne and Bella Hadid making pouty faces, all stuck on with gold magnets. Makeup and jewelry line the built-in island in the middle of the room, lit up like Sephora.

"I saw you drooling over that dress," Caroline calls back. "What kind of friend would I be if I didn't let you try it on?"

I smile, not because of the More Expensive Than My

Parents' Car ball gown I'm about to try on, but because the darling of New York Webber Academy just said she was my friend. I've been tutoring her in science every Thursday afternoon for over a year, and of course I'd hoped it would evolve into a friendship, but this is the first time she's actually said that word out loud. I have to tell Pari about this. I wonder if she'll be jealous. Or intrigued.

Don't make a big deal about it, Waverly. Oh, who am I kidding? This is a Big Deal! Being in Caroline's circle is like having a key to the city—it'll get you in anywhere. And who knows? Maybe upgrading from her tutor to her friend will raise my social score.

But really, it's just nice to have friends. I've never been great at making friends. I wish I could blame it on the kids at Webber being classist snobs, but even back in public school when I was on the same level as everyone else, I always ate lunch alone. I think it's an autistic thing, but maybe it's just a me thing. A Waverly thing. Every day I worry that I'll somehow scare away the two friends I do have at Webber—Pari and Frank. So, yeah, hearing someone like Caroline call me her friend feels damn good.

I throw the heavy skirt of my school uniform onto the floor, then the itchy sweater, white shirt, and sports bra. Once I'm down to my underwear, I stare lovingly at the extravagant dress hanging on the back of the door. It's a regal red couture ball gown designed by Christian Siriano. It's too expensive for me to even look at, and I told Caroline as much when she first suggested I try it on. But once Caroline gets an idea in her head, it's pointless to fight her—especially if it means getting out of studying biology for a few minutes.

The material is smooth and cool on my skin, and it slides on like it was meant for me. I hold my breath as I gently lift it around my waist and chest. Not gonna lie, I'm afraid of it. I'm afraid of ripping it or hurting it somehow. I'm afraid I'll like wearing it so much that nothing will ever live up to this moment again. I'm afraid this is as close to Caroline's life as I'll ever get. The tulle skirt cascades down to the floor. The V-shaped neckline is embellished with little jewels that sparkle in the light.

This is nothing like my usual OOTD. When I'm not in the awful Webber Academy uniform (all dark blue and white stripes, too-tight necktie, material that bites into me), I normally avoid too-tight or potentially scratchy clothes, prioritizing comfort over style. But this dress feels almost soothing on my skin, and there aren't even any pointy tags I'd need to cut off. It's tight, but in a comforting, weighted-blanket kind of way. I never in a million years thought I'd feel comfortable in a couture ball gown, but this isn't so bad.

Caroline shrieks when I shuffle back into her room, and I worry that her dad, famous computer scientist turned billionaire entrepreneur Gregory Sinclair, is going to think I'm trying to murder her or something.

"Okay," Caroline says. "I hate that you look better in it than me, but I love it for you."

She turns me around to face the mirror while she zips up the back of the dress, and that's when I see my reflection.

Maybe it's the built-in ring light doing me favors, but I feel like royalty. I'm standing straighter, taller, like I'm proud of what the world sees when they look at me.

Is this how Caroline feels all the time?

A sharp feeling of shame rushes through me, because it shouldn't take an extravagant dress to make me feel worthy. But when you spend every day being surrounded by people who have so much more than you, it's easy to feel like you're not good enough. It's easy to equate money with worth. A lump stings my throat and I wipe at rogue tears, hopefully before Caroline notices, but she's too distracted by her phone buzzing on her desk. Her boyfriend's face flashes on the screen: Jack's trying to FaceTime her. Only his name has been changed to Jackass, which means they're fighting again. She declines it for the fifth time tonight.

"What did he do now?" I ask.

Caroline lets out a dramatic sigh. "Pretty sure he's cheating on me."

"With who?" I probably should have at least *pretended* to be surprised, but whatever. She must know, right? She deserves so much better.

She shrugs, eyes back on her phone. "No idea. But he's been doing this thing where he ghosts me for days, then suddenly calls nonstop, wasted. Like, he won't reply to my texts, but then he'll call me drunk at three A.M., rambling about how he's sorry."

"Sorry for what?"

"That's the thing," she says, running her fingers through her long, dark hair. "He won't tell me."

I honestly don't know why she's with a jerk like Jack. Caroline is the most popular girl in school, because she treats everyone like her equal—even me, the autistic, gay scholarship nerd from Queens everyone else ignores. Jack, however, is a future frat boy from a family of corrupt prescription drug peddlers who flips up the collars of his pastel polo shirts. I mean, yeah, he's good-looking in a Ken doll kinda way, but all that is ruined the moment he opens his mouth and lets his assholery spill out. I've tried to figure out why she repeatedly chooses to exchange bodily fluids with him, but it's one of life's great mysteries. Maybe this time she's truly done with him.

"I don't want to go to the boring masquerade with him," she says.

"You have to go!" I look back at my reflection, the dress spilling out around me. I'm a Disney princess. "You're going to own the night!"

"I don't *want* to own the night," she says. "I want a night of my own. Seriously, the ball, it's all cheek kisses, fake smiles, and backstabbing under the guise of fundraising for a school that already has more money than God." Caroline falls back onto the pillows of her rose-gold four-poster bed and sighs. "My queendom for a night off from all the high society bullshit."

I had no idea Caroline felt this way. I thought she loved being everyone's favorite. Even in biology class, where she struggles the most, there's practically a line of people wanting to partner with her on group assignments. It never occurred to me that she'd tire of all the attention—that she needs a break.

Webber Academy is one of the wealthiest private schools in the country. The annual Masquerade Ball is its biggest benefit of the year, raising money for the school and celebrating new members of the Dean's Society.

For people like me, a Webber Academy education opens up the whole world. It's my ticket to a good college, connections to the most powerful names in the country, and a future of financial stability for myself and my parents. Besides, the money raised at the masquerade goes to the Webber Foundation, and from there it's given to local nonprofits and allocated to the scholarship program. It's not like the dean pockets it for himself.

Dean Owen Webber always says that, at the academy, we are a family, but as much as I want to believe I'm in the family, it's hard not to feel left out when the cheapest tickets to the masquerade are still ten thousand bucks—obviously, scholarship kids need not apply. I've always dreamed about walking into the Masquerade Ball and seeing it with my own eyes. To maybe even be invited to join the Dean's Society for who I am, instead of what I have. The night is shrouded in mystery; everyone hands in their phones and cameras at the door. The only photos are taken by approved photographers, and even then, only a select few of the images are posted online. The exclusivity is part of the allure.

"Do you know what I would give to go to that ball?" I ask

her, a little too desperately. "You have no idea how lucky you are. I'd have to tutor every kid in school for years and probably sell an organ to afford that ticket."

Truth is, tutoring doesn't come easily to me. I have a learning disability, dyscalculia, which makes numbers and equations basically impossible for my brain to process—my calculator is my best friend. But people assume that being autistic means I'm some kind of genius, and classmates started offering me hundreds of dollars to tutor them, so I agreed. I already have to work twice as hard as everyone else to keep up anyway, may as well get paid for it. I mainly tutor in English and bio, my favorite subjects. I read ahead a little, memorize as much of the texts as I can, spend a few extra hours a week studying while the rich kids are weekending at their summer houses, and voilà. The infinity of online study guides helps, too, and the extra time I've spent trying to beef up my tutoring skills has even boosted my own grades, as well as my Venmo account. Everybody wins.

"You worry about money too much," she says.

My skin bristles. It's not the first time she's said that to me. I heard it when she invited me out to some party in East Williamsburg, when the only way to get there was three different trains that would take two hours, or a Lyft, which I couldn't afford. I heard it again when she asked why I don't just buy Starbucks on the way to school instead of bringing instant coffee in my dad's old thermos. I try to soften my tone when I say, "That's what happens when you don't have it."

Caroline presses her lips into a hard line, and I worry I've offended her. Oh, man, I hope I didn't just get demoted from friend status.

"Anyway." I pick up my bio book from her desk. "We really need to focus. We still have one more chapter in this section and it took me three reads before I fully grasped it. I'll go get changed."

Caroline looks at me with pity. "Waverly, you work harder than any of the trust-fundians at school. And you put up with their one-percenter shit on top of it. I don't know how you deal."

One day I'll be rich, and I'll have my own designer gowns in my closet, and I'll never take them for granted. But most important, I'll be a doctor, an expert in neurology, and I'll be helping people.

"It's not so bad," I lie. Actually, the kids at school can be truly awful. "But I wouldn't mind being you for a day."

I put my book back down and glance at Caroline, expecting to see more pity in her warm brown eyes, but instead, they're lit up in excitement. "Be careful what you wish for."

I quirk an eyebrow at her. "Huh?"

A mischievous smile squirms across her face. She stands behind me, both of us turning to face the mirror. "You're going to the ball, Cinderella."

"Again," I say, full of suspicion. "Huh?"

She laughs. "You'll wear my dress, and my mask, and go have that wild party night you deserve. Everyone will treat you like a queen."

I laugh. "I can't pass as you." Sure, we're practically the

same height and both have dark hair and pale-ass skin. But where Caroline has breasts, I have . . . not much. And her legs are longer than mine, though I guess no one would see my legs under this huge, flowing gown.

"Yeah, you can! It's a *masquerade,* genius. People will be in disguises. Besides, this dress has been all over my feed this week—they won't even question whether it's me wearing it. Our voices aren't super different, and anyway, it'll be loud, and dark, and people will be drinking. We can totally pull it off."

For a glorious moment, I let myself imagine what it would feel like to walk into the ball in this incredible dress and have everyone treat me like I paid to be there. To live Caroline's life for just one night. But I shake off the fantasy when I remember one giant ass of a problem.

"What about Jack? He's going to be there."

She shrugs like her boyfriend is a minor detail. "He knows I'm mad at him. You could ignore him all night, he'll just think I'm pissed. Also, his dad will be there, and when Dr. Bradley is around, Jack is always on his best behavior. He'll be too focused on being Daddy's special boy to pay attention to anything else. Believe me."

My heart beats a little faster. Am I really considering this? What if I get caught? It would be humiliating. Everyone would know how desperate I am to be like them, and if there's one thing worse than being on the outside it's people knowing how badly you just want to be inside. My above-it-all mask is all I have; I can't risk losing it. "No. I don't think it's a good idea, Caroline. I can't do it."

Her phone buzzes with a text, and I see on the screen that it's from Max, Caroline's BFF and resident gossip girl of Webber Academy. Max and I don't talk much, but that's mostly my fault—she's very pretty and I get tongue-tied around her. Caroline's eyes widen at the text.

"Huh," Caroline says as she reads it. "Apparently Ash flew back from London for the masquerade. I bet she's the mystery guest Webber's been talking about, this year's new Dean's Society member."

And suddenly I'm not breathing.

Ash. Ashley Webber.

Caroline doesn't know it, but Ash is my ex-girlfriend. If she ever was my girlfriend. What we had, whatever it was, we kept secret—partly because Ash isn't out, and partly because she's the daughter of Owen Webber, the founder and dean of New York Webber Academy. Neither of us wanted the kind of attention our relationship would bring. I didn't want people asking why the richest girl in school was dating the scholarship kid; they'd think I was doing it for a status upgrade. Not to mention how everyone was always in Ash's business, orbiting around her for scraps of popularity or gossip to use as social currency. With our relationship, I think she wanted something sacred and private and special. For a while, that was me. I was her sacred, special thing. And she was mine.

And then she was gone.

All I have left to remind me of her now is the heartache. No matter what I do, no matter how much time passes, the hurt just won't go away. Pari says I'm holding on to her too tight still, waiting for her to come back to me, and I've always denied it. But now, Ash is back in New York. My heart is racing. Palms sweating. Maybe this is what I've been holding on for this whole time, one more chance. With her.

"I'll go."

"Where?" Caroline says, already reabsorbed in her phone.

I can't believe I'm saying these words out loud. "I'll go to the masquerade in your place."

Caroline lights up. "Yes, Cinderella!"

I keep admiring myself in the mirror while she fetches the mask from the safe—yes, an actual safe—in her closet. It's wrapped in bloodred tissue paper inside a metallic gold box, and I've been dying to see it in real life instead of just on Instagram.

"Here it is," she says as she lifts the lid off. "The *pièce de résistance.*"

It's a shimmering gold mask with holes for the eyes, nostrils, and mouth. Lines have been carved into it, giving it eerie facial features, feminine and delicate. Otherworldly and somehow fae. But what really makes it stand out are the thin golden rods on top of it, forming a crown. It looks like something that would be worn by an ancient sun goddess—or a celebrity going to Coachella.

"The crown has flecks of real gold in it." Caroline gently places the mask over my face, ties the ribbon tight so it stays firm, and steps back to take in the full sight of me. "Perfection."

"There's no way I'll blend in on the subway in this outfit," I say, thinking of trying to get to the ball from Queens.

"No way," she says, shaking her head. "You're not wearing this on the subway. In fact, you're not even carrying it on the train tonight. It's too bulky, and I'd die before letting it touch the grimy floor of the R train."

"It'll be fine," I say. "My mom and I once rode the subway with an armchair we found on the street."

Caroline makes a face.

My cheeks warm. "It was a really nice chair."

She shrugs. "You'll take our town car home tonight. I'll call Bruce." Before I can argue, she's on the phone asking her family's driver to be ready to take me home in thirty minutes. I retreat back to her walk-in to step out of the dress and back into my uniform, and together we place it back in its fancy garment bag.

"Now." Caroline claps her hands together. "I'm going to give you a lesson on How to Be Moi, so pay attention."

I chuckle while I pull my sweater over my head. "I think I've got that down. All I gotta do is flip my hair every now and then and slip French words into every sentence. Instant bougie bitch."

She gasps, making a big show of being offended. "*Pardonnez-moi, mademoiselle?* Says you, with your closet full of flannel shirts and nails bitten down to nothing—you're a walking lesbian stereotype."

I stumble backward and clutch my heart dramatically. "*Moi?*"

Laughter spills out of both of us, but then Caroline turns stone cold. "Seriously, though. Just because I want a break from this world doesn't mean I want to be ostracized from it. I have a reputation to uphold, a vibe that people do and should expect from me. You need to make them believe in that journey."

She starts listing things off, counting on her fingers as she does. "I don't smile. Ever. But you'll be wearing a mask so that shouldn't be a problem. I avoid eye contact with teachers, and pretty much all adults, because, honestly, who has the energy to deal with them? But hey, that should be easy for you with the autism stuff, right?"

On the outside, I smile and nod, but on the inside, I wince and shrink. It's not that she's wrong; eye contact is hard for me, but it doesn't feel right that she gets to say it like that. There's no way I could ever tell her that, though, because she's Caroline, and besides, I don't even understand why it makes me feel so prickly, so how could I make someone else understand?

"Your posture needs work," she says, her gaze dragging down my body. "You're all hunched up at the shoulders like you're trying to crawl into a ball and hide."

Called out.

I straighten my spine in a way that feels unnatural and vulnerable.

"Much better," Caroline says. "If we had more time, I'd send you to the modeling class I took when I was eleven, just to get a quick download on how to walk and pose." She sighs. "But this will do."

I'm feeling more like a monkey in a science experiment every second. But then I think about walking into the Webber Academy ball, how everyone will adore me, wish they were me, how I'll be the star for just one night . . . and how Ash will be there to see me shine. It's just one night.

Caroline crosses her room, searches her Spotify playlists, and hits play. Shitty club music fills the room from the speakers in the ceiling. It's too loud for me, but I don't say anything. "It's time," she says with an evil smile. "Show me what you've got."

I spend the next twenty minutes walking back and forth down the length of her giant bedroom. "Less slouching," she orders on my fifty millionth circuit of the room. "More strutting."

Next, I practice talking and laughing like her, and even though it's definitely a work in progress, I'm not half bad. We've been spending every Thursday after school together for a year now, so I've had a lot of study time. Besides, being autistic in an ableist world means learning how to mimic other people's behavior as a way to fit in. It's called masking—suppressing my natural autistic traits so that I can pass as a neurotypical person. Resisting the urge to rock back and forth during class, or tap my hands on my desk, or count how many stairs I climb out loud. Hiding my anxiety and discomfort when people get too close, or too loud, or too confusing. Pretending I'm fine when I'm completely overwhelmed and watching the clock for the lunch bell to ring so I can disappear into the bathroom, pop my earplugs in, and bury my head in my arms until I can breathe again.

It's a survival mechanism, like a chameleon changing its colors to hide from predators, only a lot less cool and way more exhausting.

When Caroline is satisfied that I sound enough like her to fool her friends in a loud, music-filled ballroom, we move on to the final step: a Caroline-style selfie—from above, angled to the right, chin slightly turned to the left, eyes sultry behind the mask. I take a dozen different shots. Then she picks her favorite and rolls it through three different photo editing apps to get the lighting and colors just right so it matches her aesthetic.

"I'll post this before the party," she says. "It'll look like I'm getting ready in real time."

I grin at her. "You're an evil genius."

She giggles, placing a hand on her cheek. "Stop! You're making me blush."

That's when the buzzer rings, and she hurries me out of her room. "That's Bruce. See you at school, Cinderella!"

I creep down the stairs as quietly as possible, cradling the dress and mask box like a newborn baby, but stop cold when I hear Caroline's dad yell in his office, "Stop!"

I freeze. For a heart-stopping moment, I think he's screaming at me. Oh, god. He thinks I'm stealing the dress. I turn to look at him in his office, but his back is to me. Then I hear a muffled voice yelling about "*Cassandra!*," and I realize Gregory is on the phone.

"We should have told someone," he hisses. "Now it's too late, and people will suffer."

His voice bounces off the walls. I've only spoken to Caroline's father a handful of times, but he's been nothing but kind and very soft-spoken, almost shy. He's always by Dean Webber's side at school events; I think they've been close friends for years. I've never heard him yell like this.

Gregory turns around and spots me. Our eyes lock. Then he crosses the room and shuts the door in my face, drowning out the rest of the conversation.

CHAPTER TWO

Our old Toyota whines as it slugs across the Queensboro Bridge into Manhattan. Every day, I fully expect it to give up right in the middle of early-morning traffic. It's been known to break down at the absolute worst possible times, usually when my mom has a doctor's appointment she's been waiting months for or I have an important exam to get to. The front passenger's-side window doesn't close fully, and the duct-tape system my dad came up with to fix it is starting to give up, so my big headphones are a must when we're faced with the blasting wind and constant car-honking of the bridge. They're not noise-canceling—those are expensive—but they help.

My dad sits behind the wheel, his balding head gently nodding along to some song from his youth, only ever singing the chorus because he can't remember the rest of the lyrics. Every now and then I catch him glancing over at my mom, his brow crinkled with worry as she massages the joints of her hands. She hasn't had a pain flare in ages, but the price of her medication tripled a few months ago, and she had to stop taking it. And it's started to show—a worsening limp from the pain in her knees and ankles; migraines forcing her to miss work; more frequent memory lapses; and then, this morning, she dug her old compression gloves out of her dresser drawer.

Mom was diagnosed with relapsing-remitting multiple sclerosis about a year and a half ago, but she'd been experiencing fatigue, tremors, and pain flares for as long as I've been alive. It took over a decade of trying to get doctors to listen to her before someone finally took her seriously.

My childhood is filled with memories of being babysat by neighbors in the middle of the night while my dad rushed my mom to the ER with a migraine so painful she started vomiting, days when her pain was so bad she couldn't get out of bed, sitting with her in the waiting rooms of doctors, psychologists, chiropractors—anyone who might be able to help ease her pain that would still be covered by our health insurance plan.

She had almost given up on finding a doctor. All they did was condescend to her, tell her it was all in her head, or prescribe medications that didn't work and then blame her for their failures. I couldn't understand why no one believed her, why the fact that she said she was in constant pain wasn't enough for them. If they couldn't see it on their scans or in their textbooks, then it didn't exist to them.

So, when I was about twelve, I decided I would become a doctor, but I'd be different from all the rest. I'd believe my patients when they told me about their pain, instead of dismissing them based on their gender or race or weight. I researched the best premed schools in the country, chose Yale as my first preference, then googled which New York schools had the highest acceptance rate.

Wasting no time, and with my parents' enthusiastic encouragement, I applied to the Webber Academy Uplift Program (read: scholarships for kids who "show potential and ambition, but are unable to attain a high-quality education due to personal or financial hardship") and got in. Now, in my senior year, I'm right on track for Yale, which would grease the tracks for the Yale School of Medicine, work as a neurologist, and the life I know I'm supposed to lead.

But it's not just my education that Webber Academy provides. Once Dean Webber heard about my mom's health struggles, he connected her with specialists who not only believed her, but gave her the answers she'd spent over a decade searching for.

Webber, the man and the school, is basically my family's saving grace now. Hard to get too reverse-snobby about a place when it's quite literally your whole life.

My dad reaches a hand over to take Mom's, and she offers a forced smile as he rubs it for her. None of us have admitted it out loud yet, but it's obvious her pain is getting worse by the day, and without her meds, there's nothing we can do about it.

It lights a fire in my belly.

"Dean Webber would help pay for the medi—" I start to say once we're over the bridge, but my mom stops me.

"No," she snaps. "He's done enough for us. I don't want to take advantage of his kindness."

I bite my tongue to stop myself from arguing with her. The last thing I want is to be the reason her pain flares even more. But if the dean knew, he would want to help, I know he would.

The car groans as we pull into the underground parking garage of Webber Academy, and I feel like groaning, too. The first moments before walking into school are the most anxiety-provoking for me, when my stomach twists itself into nauseated knots and my hands shake, but part of my scholarship is dependent on my attendance record, so I can't afford to miss a day. That, and my parents would be furious. They go in to Webber Academy every day, too—my dad as a custodian and my mom as a chef in the kitchen—and they do it for me. For my education, and for my future.

Some of the kids at school have "joked" that I got the Indentured Servitude Program, because my parents work at the school. But I got into Webber on my own, and it wasn't until later that the dean gave my parents jobs out of the goodness of his heart. He knew we had hit hard times and wanted to help, so that I could focus on my studies. That's how much he believes in me.

In the parking garage, my parents kiss me goodbye, then take the service elevator while I walk up the tree-lined side path to the main campus. I hold my anxiety in my lungs as I join the other kids streaming up the path, putting on my Resting Apathy Face. The more I pretend I don't care what they think of me, the more they leave me alone. The thought crosses my mind that they might finally notice me at the masquerade, only they won't really know it's me. I wonder if that's better or worse.

Before I can decide, I notice my footsteps echoing more loudly than usual. Something feels different this morning. The campus center foyer is quieter. The boys aren't doing their macho morning ritual of punching each other in the nads. People are whispering in small groups of three or four. Even teachers are being weird. I peer into one of the classrooms as I pass and see Mrs. Carter, my English teacher, dabbing a tissue under her eyes like she's been crying.

What the hell is going on?

Pari, my best friend, is waiting for me on our usual couch in the student lounge, scrolling and eating a Reese's Peanut Butter Cup. I let out a soft sigh, relieved to see at least she's acting like her normal self. Her long black hair is tied into a high ponytail that would rival Ariana Grande's, and her long fingernails are painted neon yellow with hints of glitter. A matching yellow eyeliner traces the rims of her eyelids, popping brilliantly against her brown skin, and definitely breaking school dress code—something she always manages to get away with. By now the faculty have learned not to argue with her, lest they face the wrath of one of her "woke rants," as Mr. Cameron called them once in biology class. Her cane leans against the couch, which means she's having a bad pain day. Pari has a rad collection of canes, and today it's her leopard-print one, matching the yellow on her nails and eyes perfectly.

I see Frank across the room, on his way over to us. Frank is my very own personal computer geek, with thick glasses, pasty white skin that burns even on the cloudiest day, and a penchant for *Doctor Who* Reddit threads. His name is actually Francis, but he prefers Frank, like his dad, whom he was named after. He worries his TONY WAS RIGHT lapel pin as he lopes our way, grinning, laptop tucked under one arm.

"Hey, Fransissy!" Lance Howard, a Stanford hopeful and the son of a big Wall Street guy, calls to Frank as he passes. Frank looks over and instantly catches one of his enormous feet on a table leg. The rest happens in slow motion. Frank lurches forward, falling hard on his knees; his laptop falls out of his grasp, skidding across the tiled floor.

Lance and his jerk friends laugh their asses off. Pari has her cane in her hand and is on her feet, moving quickly.

"Are you okay?" I ask as I help Frank up. He nods, but I can tell by his tomato-colored cheeks that he's embarrassed.

"Hey, dickwad!" Pari storms over to Lance. He's got at least three inches on her, but she shoves the wrapper of her Peanut Butter Cup into his mouth. "If you're gonna talk trash, you're gonna eat it, too."

Frank and I make our way over, prepared to back her up.

Lance spits the wrapper out while his buddies laugh. He glances down at Pari's cane and kicks it. She loses her balance for a second, but catches herself before she falls.

"My bad," he says. "Didn't see it."

Frank and I stand on either side of Pari.

"Don't you have contraband Adderall to snort?" I say to him.

He snarls at me and throws the Peanut Butter Cup wrapper at my feet. "Don't you have trash to pick up? Just like your dad?"

Then he and his buddies walk away, laughing.

"Asshole!" Pari calls after him.

"I swear to god," Frank says through gritted teeth. "If I wasn't on scholarship . . ."

Someone clears their throat behind us. The three of us turn to see Mr. Cameron staring us down, his white mustache twitching.

"That's hardly the language of a young lady," he says to Pari, then turns to Frank. "And Francis, threats of violence? What would your father think?"

Pari's jaw drops. "Sir, didn't you see what Lance did?"

"What I saw was you cursing in the middle of the hallway." He checks the time on his watch. "It's a hard morning for all of us here, so I'll let it slide. But any more outbursts from any of you three today and it's detention."

I swallow hard, and I see Frank's shoulders tense. Like he said, he's a scholarship kid, too. Detention for us could put our whole education at risk.

"Yes, sir," I sputter out. "Sorry, sir."

Frank straightens his blazer. "Won't happen again."

I can practically feel Pari rolling her eyes at us, but her parents are what you might call Top Tier Donors. She can afford trouble in ways we can't—and sometimes I think she seeks it out. The way people constantly underestimate her, I don't blame her. People see her cane and assume she's made of glass—or worse, they tell her she's inspiring. Last year we went to a disability-rights rally with my parents, and Pari gave my mom a button that said NOT YOUR INSPIRATION PORN, and my mom wears it everywhere now.

"You okay?" I ask her.

She lifts her cane up to inspect the damage. "He scuffed Michael Cane." Pari named her mobility aid after the British actor Michael Caine, because she's a sucker for puns, just like me. She has hypermobile Ehlers-Danlos syndrome, which means sometimes her joints slip out of place and her body hurts a lot. That's my basic understanding of it, anyway. She doesn't always use her cane, but when she does I know she's probably dealing with a ton of invisible pain—just like my mom does.

She turns to Frank. "You've got to stand up for yourself more, dude."

He checks his laptop for damage. "Trust me, I'm doing them a favor by restraining myself. Besides, one day they'll be working for me." He doesn't meet her gaze, probably embarrassed she came to his defense for the umpteenth time. Pari isn't just a girl to Frank, she's The Girl. He's been hopelessly in love with her since he showed up for his first day at Webber our junior year, and it's the worst-kept secret in the world. He pretends he's not infatuated with her, and she pretends she doesn't notice the way he looks at her.

Frank and I initially bonded as fellow Uplift Program kids. He's a math wiz and a chess champion from Brooklyn, where his family owned one of the oldest pizza places in the city. But with the storms getting worse the last few years, the restaurant kept flooding, the damage was too expensive, and they had to close. Then his dad died of a heart attack the same week. It made the news, and Dean Webber heard about it and reached out to offer Frank Junior a scholarship on the spot, as a second chance for him and his family.

The three of us kind of fell in together as a way to survive being different. *We are the weirdos, mister.*

Suddenly, something Mr. Cameron says replays in my mind. "What did Cameron mean when he said it's a hard day?" Pari and Frank exchange a glance. "What?"

Pari pulls me in closer and shows me something on her phone. It's an article in *The New York Times.*

Tech Billionaire Found Unconscious
in Manhattan Apartment

Forty-three-year-old Gregory Sinclair was reportedly found in his home office by the housekeeper early this morning. He is currently in critical condition at Lenox Hill Hospital. The family's lawyer says he is unlikely to recover.

My chest tightens. "Oh, no. Caroline. I just saw him last night." My voice is barely a whisper. My mind spins. His voice echoes in my head: *People will suffer.*

The first bell rings, making me jump. I tell Pari and Frank I'll see them later—at least I think I do—then hazily walk to homeroom.

Caroline's empty seat may as well have a neon sign above it, the way people keep casting concerned glances at it.

Caroline's best friend, Max, sits at the far end of the

classroom with the rest of her homeroom squad. "Has anyone heard from her? She won't reply to my texts." Max, one of only a handful of Black students in my year, is the daughter of a prominent sustainability professor at The New School, and her dad is a neurosurgeon who went to the same school I want to go to.

"Same," Alice, another of Caroline's friends, says. "I even tried calling her, but her phone's off." Alice, well, she scares me. She's a ballerina, thin and tall with porcelain-white skin and a kind of intensity that vibrates off of her. Her dad is a congressman who makes frequent problematic appearances on cable news shows that he then has to apologize for on different cable news shows. When I turn eighteen, the first thing I'm doing is voting him out.

Max's brow furrows. "This is so fucked up."

Alice leans in closer, looking around before she speaks. I avert my gaze. "Do you think he . . . I mean, I heard it was pills. Was it on purpose?"

My stomach goes sour. Pills? The image of Mr. Sinclair in his office last night returns to the forefront of my mind. I was so focused on getting out of there with Caroline's dress that I ignored how agitated he was. What if I was the last person to see him conscious?

I shake that question away. No. Surely, Caroline saw him after I left. Even just to say good night.

"Poor Caroline," Max says, mirroring my thoughts exactly.

· · ·

By the time lunch rolls around, the weight in the air has lightened to a low mist and the rumors have spread, working their way through the student body like rot.

"Maybe it was some kind of Russian spy hit," a freshman says to his friends as I pass by. "Old Greg got in too deep with some Putin shit or something."

I roll my eyes.

"I heard he never got over his wife leaving him," a girl says to her friends. "I mean, Caroline never talks about her mom. That's weird, right?"

Not weird. Sometimes it's easier to just never talk about the things that hurt most.

I walk into the student café and join the line. Mom is working today, and if I can catch a glimpse of her in the kitchen, maybe she'll sneak me a chocolate mousse.

"I get that it's sad," says Alice, who's a few people ahead of me, talking to Lance. Alice is nice enough when she's alone, but something happens when she's with Lance. She turns mean, and together the two of them stoke the cruelty in each other. Sometimes it's me on the other end of their flames, but today Caroline is in everyone's crosshairs. "It's tragic, obviously. But Caroline would want the show to go on, you know? She's strong like that."

Someone sighs behind me, and I turn to see Max shaking her head. "Can you believe her?"

For a second I don't answer, because I don't realize she's talking to me. "Unfortunately, yes."

"You're right, Alice," Max calls, then leaves her place in line to face down the other girl. Even though Max likes to gossip, she's also Caroline's most loyal friend. "We wouldn't want the near death of our friend's father to get in the way of a good time."

"I just meant—"

"We all know what you meant," she says as she flips her dark bob of curls.

Alice shrivels, and I'm glad Caroline has someone looking out for her. The whole line is staring in our direction now, and even though I'm not the focus, I'm way too close for comfort. I slide my tray back and get out of there. My stomach hurts from the tension. I'll eat later.

I find Pari and Frank at our usual table by the windows. The sun shines through from Seventy-First Street, casting them in a warm glow. Outside, the trees are growing greener the further into spring we get. Prewar brownstones stand proudly on the other side of the street, maids and nannies in the windows while the owners are at work. My thoughts go back to Caroline, how she's only a few blocks away, probably sitting by her father's hospital bed.

And that's when it hits me—with Gregory in the hospital, there's no way Caroline's plan to have me play her stand-in at the ball is happening. Which means my hopes of seeing Ash have turned to dust. I sink against Pari and fold myself over the table, covering my face with my arms.

"Same," Pari says, then rubs my back.

I groan. I want to stay here and hide in the dark forever.

This is why I don't let myself get my hopes up about things. It always ends in disappointment.

Gasps echo around the room, and I peek from my hiding place. The flat-screens on every wall have sparked to life. Dean Webber sits at the wide mahogany desk in his office on the top floor of the school, hands clasped in front of him. His salt-and-pepper hair is perfectly combed, his sharp jaw tight and blue eyes somber. It's like a presidential address.

"Good afternoon, Webber Academy," he says. "I'm sure by now you've all heard the terribly sad news about Gregory Sinclair. He is a dear friend of mine, a valued member of our Webber family. So much of what we have built here is thanks to him. All of us here are hoping for a swift recovery, and keeping his daughter, our dear Caroline, in our thoughts and prayers."

His face lifts, and his mouth turns up into a warm, reassuring smile. "Now, I know you're all wondering how this will affect the annual Webber Academy Masquerade Ball."

People perk up. What little conversation there was quiets.

"Like I always say, here at Webber, we are a family," Dean Webber continues. "And like all families, when we are hit with hardship, we pull *together*. When we have big dreams, and we all work hard to achieve them, we don't let anything get in the way of that. We don't let anything get in the way of what we want. It's the Webber way."

Someone cheers and a few people clap, sincerely.

"So, after discussion with the senior faculty," Webber says, "I've decided that the Masquerade Ball will go on tonight as planned. Not only that, it will be held in honor of my dear friend, Gregory Sinclair."

Now people really cheer. The sounds of excited squeals and low-key high fives fill the air.

"I look forward to seeing you all at the ball. I've overseen a complete remodeling of the Sewing Factory especially for your enjoyment. I guarantee it will be a night none of us will forget. Thank you, and learn well."

The televisions go black, reflecting the celebrating student body now. I glance over to where Max and the rest of Caroline's social group sit. Alice sits straight, a look of triumph on her face. Then I spot Jack, Caroline's boyfriend, crouched over the table, dark circles under his eyes like he hasn't slept in days. He looks thoroughly depressed. Maybe he has a heart after all. Or, more likely, he's hungover from another night in the Meatpacking District with his friends.

"I heard Ash Webber is going to be there," says Lance. He nudges Jack, who doesn't even flinch. "Dude, girls coming back from college? You know they're down for a casual thing. I'm totally shooting my shot tonight."

Pari turns to me and smirks. She's the only one who knows about me and Ash, and she enthusiastically volunteered to be our alibi while we went on dates. "Any opportunity to further the queer agenda," she'd said, grinning wide.

God, I miss those days. How Ash and I would find a quiet spot in the bird sanctuary in Central Park and just sit there for hours. Talking, kissing, taking selfies that were just for us. She'd name the birds that sang in the branches above us, and I'd nervously watch her react to the playlist I'd spent hours making for her. We'd be sitting in the middle of Manhattan, but it felt like the whole island had gone dark, and it was ours alone.

A selfish thought crosses my mind. Would going to the ball disguised as Caroline anyway make me a terrible person? Is it disrespectful and gross to go through with our plan even while she's by her dad's hospital bed? Of course it is.

My mind swings back and forth between going and not going. I pull out my phone to text Caroline and ask her what I should do, but she hasn't replied to my earlier text sending my best to her and her dad. She has too much going on right now for me to bother her with this.

I need a second and third opinion. I wave Pari and Frank closer until we're huddled over the table. "I have to tell you something," I say in a low voice. "But you can't tell *anyone,* okay?"

"Sure," Pari says.

"Who am I gonna tell?" Frank says with a shrug. "You're the only two people I talk to."

I give him a serious look. "Frank."

"Okay, okay," he says. "Scout's honor. Now come on, spill it."

I take in a deep breath. "Last night, when I was at Caroline's place tutoring, she asked me to go to the masquerade in her place." Pari and Frank both furrow their brows. "Like, disguised as her."

"Why would she ask you to do that?" Frank asks. "She loves that shit."

I shrug my shoulders. "I thought so, too, but she said she's sick of it. And she's fighting with Jack. She wanted a night off from her life, basically."

"So," Pari says, eyes wide, "what did you say?"

"Well, at first I said no, but then . . ." Frank doesn't know about me and Ash, so I trail off. "I tried the dress on, and it looked so good. So I changed my mind."

Pari claps her hands excitedly. "Yesssss! I love this for us!"

I grab her hands and hold them still. "No, I can't go now. Not with her dad in a freaking coma." There's a pause, and I add in my quietest voice, "Can I?"

Pari slaps her hands onto my cheeks and looks me dead in the eyes.

"You have to do this," she says, her voice serious. She turns to Frank. "Tell her she has to do this."

He looks uncertain, but he'd never disobey Pari. "Hey, I like a good caper."

"But Caroline—"

"Shhh!" She presses her index finger over my lips. "Caroline is a wild card. Everyone knows she likes to shock people. No one would expect her to show up at the ball, and that's exactly why they wouldn't be surprised when you, aka Caroline, do just that."

I narrow my eyes as I try to follow Pari's train of logic. She lets me go, and I stare down at my bitten-down fingernails, mulling it over. The bell rings, and Frank is up in a flash, never wanting to be late to class. Pari and I lag behind him, and she nudges me with her elbow.

"Please come," she says. "Frank scored a free ticket from

Webber, and I know he wants us to go together. Like, *together* together. But if you come, you and I can get ready together and I can avoid everyone thinking Frank and I are on a date— especially Frank."

"Wait." That doesn't make sense. "Webber just gave Frank a ticket? Why? When? Frank didn't say—"

Pari averts her gaze. "He didn't want you to feel left out. But you're coming now, so yay!"

My chest tightens. I don't like it when my friends keep things from me. But I don't want to make a big deal out of it, so I try to forget it. "Why would the dean just give away a ticket that normally costs ten thousand dollars?"

She shrugs. "Who knows why rich white dudes do anything. Maybe Frank is the virgin sacrifice of the night and this was the only way to lure him there."

I snort back laughter.

A few feet away, Frank turns to give us a side-eye. "What are you laughing at?"

"Nothing," Pari and I sing in unison, then burst into more giggles.

Sigh. It would be pretty sweet to have a fun night out with my friends for once. With Frank gaining speed ahead of us, I tug on Pari's elbow and pull her in closer.

"Ash is going," I say. "That's why I said yes to Caroline's plan. I want to talk to her. I have to."

Pari nods. "Talk as in confront her for ghosting you and breaking your heart? Or talk as in beg her to take you back? Because I'm afraid I can't let you do the latter."

I chew on my bottom lip. "No begging. I swear. But can't there be a happy medium? Maybe she has a really good explanation for leaving."

She gives me a look that says *oh, honey.* "Listen." Pari stops and I stop with her. "You've been heartsick over her for almost a year, so I agree that you should talk to her. Closure is healthy. Dr. Donna says so." Dr. Donna is Pari's therapist. "But Ash abandoned you. She dropped you like you were nothing and literally fled the country."

I wince at that, but she's right. "But I want to know why."

"And you deserve that," she says. "You do. But whether or not you get those answers at the ball, after tonight, that has to be it. No more pining, no more wondering, no more waiting for Ash to come back for good."

"No loitering, girls," Mr. Cameron says as he walks by. "Don't want to be late for class."

Pari gives him an exaggerated salute. "Sir, yes, sir!"

He ignores her and keeps walking, while Pari and I try to tamp down our laughter.

Yes. This is what I want more of. What I need more of. Fun with my friends. A night off from tutoring, studying, and sitting at home alone.

Once Cameron is gone, Pari turns serious again. "Promise me that after tonight, this mess with Ash will be over for real."

"I promise." I know she's just looking out for me, but my gut tells me there really is a good reason Ash left the way she did. I don't know what it is, but I'm going to find out.

CHAPTER THREE

Thanks for the ride, Daddy," Pari says as we pull up to the cracked curb outside my building. Pari is worried I'll panic at the last minute and skip the ball, so she's decided we are getting ready together—at my place.

Judging by her dad's wrinkled brow, he isn't too pleased with that idea. "Are you sure you don't want to get ready at home?" He looks at me. "You are welcome to come, too, Waverly."

I give him a polite smile, but Pari interjects before I can answer. "We're fine, Dad."

He holds his palms up in a sign of defeat, but he keeps casting concerned glances around my neighborhood like he's afraid his Tesla is going to get carjacked any second. An old mattress has been propped up against the tree outside, along with boxes of free books and broken shelves. If Pari and her dad weren't here, I'd totally riffle through the books to see if there are any gems.

I've lived in Sunnyside my whole life. It's changed a lot since I was a kid and I've heard my parents complain about the rent going up more than once, but we know our neighbors and our favorite places know us, too. On Saturdays I walk over to the library, pick up a book order, then walk down to Calvary Cemetery, sit in my usual spot under a sprawling oak tree on a hill that overlooks Manhattan, and read all day.

I know everyone thinks their borough is the best borough in New York, but I get a special kind of defensive when folks like Pari's dad stick their nose up at Queens. He's one of those white men who think they're down-to-earth, a man of the people, but get weird when they're faced with "the people" in real life. I guess when you come from old money, live in a doorman building, and never venture out of the Upper East Side, these noisy, busy blocks feel like another world. The real world, IMO. Like, sorry we don't have any Real Housewives in the neighborhood, but we have AOC as our local rep. Can't beat that.

Pari's mom grew up in India and met her dad while they were both studying at Yale. Pari's dad's the upper-class New England type who wears sweaters around his shoulders and boat shoes everywhere. Pari, with her intersectional feminist politics and Greta Thunberg T-shirts, clashes with him on the regular, but the love is there.

"Have a safe flight," Pari says before kissing her dad on the cheek. He's headed straight to JFK for a work trip to London for the weekend. He's always jetting off to important places for important meetings with important people. And Pari's mom refuses to attend the ball, because she says the white mothers of Webber Academy are the WASPy Housewives of New York.

Once we're inside my building, we walk the four flights up, nodding to Mr. and Mrs. Lee as they cook with their door open, and the Rivera kids play in the hall.

Sarah Pawson and Cat Blanchett, my two tabby cats, greet us at the door when we walk in, circling around our ankles and meowing loudly. My mom has a doctor's appointment in the city after work, so she and my dad won't be home until we've left, and I'm grateful. The last thing I want to do is explain why I suddenly have a ticket to the ball—and an expensive dress to match.

I clench and unclench my fists as Pari takes in my tiny, comfy home. We don't have guests over very often, so whenever someone other than my parents is in the space, it feels strange. It's like worlds colliding.

The sofa bed is stretched out and unmade. Normally, my parents would fold it up before we left for school, but finding Mom's compression gloves took priority this morning, and it went undone. Our apartment is only a one-bedroom, so I sleep on the sofa. It used to be the other way around—them on the sofa bed and me in the bedroom—but once Mom's pain flares started getting worse, I finally convinced them to switch so she could be more comfortable.

I quickly step into the cramped kitchen and open the fridge, offering Pari some soda or juice, but she declines. She's more interested in the photo gallery on the wall behind the TV. Photos of me in every possible phase of my life—diaper-wearing baby, kindergartner in a Dora the Explorer T-shirt, preteen at a One Direction concert that my parents surprised me with for my tenth birthday, and a photo of me in my Webber Academy uniform, forcing a smile for my proud mom and dad.

I shouldn't feel so exposed right now. Pari has seen all this before. But still, she seems so out of place in this little corner of my life. She might be my best friend, but this is only the third time I've had the courage to invite her past the threshold of my building.

After another minute, Pari points to the One Direction concert photo and grins. "I know who we're listening to while we get ready."

She pulls up the latest Harry Styles on her phone. I kick some laundry under the sofa bed while she isn't looking and move the stack of YA novels I borrowed from the Queens Public Library off the armchair so she can sit down. If I'd known company was coming today, I would have put more effort into tidying up.

She lays her dress down on top of my comforter and drops her backpack onto the carpet. "Let's see that dress!"

I smile and walk over to the hallway closet, where I sneakily hid my dress behind our winter coats—right before I told my folks I have two separate tutoring gigs tonight in Manhattan so they won't worry about me being so late. Pari takes the dress from me and holds it up by the living room window, her hands running over the material.

"Wow," she says. "Caroline must have dropped some coin on this bad girl."

"It's Christian Siriano," I say, a little smug.

Pari's eyebrows shoot up to her hairline. "Okay, a lot of coin." She lays it gently on the bed next to hers, then claps her hands together. "We need a mirror and good lighting if I'm going to do your makeup."

We step into the bathroom, which has the best light in the whole apartment. I move my mom's CBD creams and over-the-counter pain relief meds off the sink to make room for Pari's vast collection of cosmetics. There's Fenty, MAC, Glossier, brushes and sponges and wands and oils. I'm feeling major envy of Pari's colorful, glittery palettes and professional-grade contour sticks. It's like she has all of Sephora in her bag.

She points to the closed lid of the toilet. "Sit."

I do as she asks and remain there while she dabs at my face with every tool in her box. My eyes must widen when she pulls out her dark eye shadow palette, because she smirks and says, "Remember, you're not you tonight. You're Caroline, and Caroline goes bold or goes home. Besides, your eyes are gonna be the only visible part of your face. We want them to pop!"

"Go bold or go home," I repeat, like it's a spell I'm casting on myself.

Harry Styles serenades us as we sit in my cramped bathroom. The cats saunter in curiously, then fall asleep between our feet.

"Maybe I should forget the whole law school thing," Pari

says as she applies a fresh layer of glitter to my eyelids. "Dedicate my life to makeup tutorials instead."

"I'd hit that follow button so fast," I say.

She laughs. "Can you imagine my dad's reaction?" She lowers her voice to do an impression of him. "'I didn't pay all that money to Owen Webber for my daughter to paint her face on the internet!'"

We both laugh. Pari jokes, but she's kind of a big deal online. It started with quick TikTok videos about disability and then a few trends later she was viral. I lost count of how many followers she has now, but it's in the hundreds of thousands.

"Okay, princess," she says. "Peep at your reflection, and prepare to be blown away by how damn hot you look."

I stand up and face the mirror, and my jaw drops. It's like one of those exaggerated Instagram filters has been permanently placed over my face. Turns out I actually have cheekbones? Who knew! The creams and powders feel heavy on my skin, but I remind myself that it's just for a few hours, and damn, I look good. My lips look fuller, my brows are thicker, and my eyes sparkle. It's a shame most of it is going to be hidden under a mask all night. But if I get even one minute alone with Ash, she'll see me like this. Goose bumps ripple over my skin at the thought.

"Well?" Pari says, impatient.

A wide smile spreads across my made-up face. "I love it. You're amazing, Pari."

She does a fake curtsy. "Why, thank you."

I lean in closer to the mirror, turning my head slightly to

see how the highlighter shimmers in the light. I don't look like myself, but that's the point.

"I need your help with one more thing," I say, grimacing. Then I search the cabinet for the sample contact lenses I got with my prescription glasses in the seventh grade. I've never used them because we'd never be able to afford them regularly, but I can't wear my glasses with the mask.

After an uncomfortable and somewhat painful ten minutes trying to stick little plastic circles onto my eyeballs, we get it done. I blink a few times, letting the lenses adjust. They're definitely expired, but it's only for a few hours, and without them I'll be walking into walls all night. Pari fixes some of the eyeliner I cried off trying to put the lenses in, and we're done.

"Wow," I say when I look in the mirror again. The bathroom cabinet is a little blurred around the edges, and so am I, from the outdated prescription, but it's not so bad. It's not like I have to do any reading tonight.

Pari laughs and pats me on the shoulder. "Embrace it."

I linger in the bathroom with Pari while she does her own makeup, like a magician performing her oldest trick. Liquid liner glides over her lids, ending in a thick wing tip. She drips gold oil under her eyes and presses it in with a heart-shaped sponge. Her dark brown contour stick drags along her cheekbones and under her jaw, outlining her features. We mostly hang out at school, so I don't often see this side of her. Neither of us are popular enough to be invited to parties, and I never have money to go out for lunch or to the movies with her, so I'm savoring this rare chance to have fun and let loose together tonight.

Ever the supportive BFF and ready to hype me up, Pari insists I get dressed first. She waits in the living room while I strap myself into my armor for the night. I take a deep breath, reach for the door, and step out, bracing myself for squealing. But instead, Pari is staring at her phone, brows knitted together.

"Wait," she says. "I'm confused."

I peer over her shoulder to look at her screen. It's a new Instagram post by Caroline, the photo she took of me in her costume at her place last time I saw her. There's no caption, but people are commenting with things like *OMG so happy you'll be there!* and *can't wait to see you babe xoxo.*

"That's me," I say to Pari. "We took that pic when we were coming up with the plan. She said she would post it today, so it would look like she's ready for the ball."

Pari smiles. "You know what this means? She's practically just given you permission to go ahead with the plan!"

I chew on my bottom lip nervously. This does make me feel slightly less like a terrible friend for going. Does Caroline really mean it? "You think so?"

She nods excitedly, but I still can't shake this sinking feeling of guilt. Like I'm taking advantage of a friend going through the worst possible thing. But why else would she post this?

Then, as though Caroline knows I'd still be unsure, my phone buzzes with a text from her.

have fun tonight cinderella xx

Oh. I should be relieved, but getting permission from Caroline leaves me with no way to back out. This is actually happening. I gulp and show Pari the text.

"See?" she says. "Now you have no choice but to go out and have the time of your life!"

I guess a part of me thought this was all too good to be true. I was waiting for the other shoe to drop, for something to happen to ruin this night. For permission to give up, take off this ridiculous costume, put on my sweats and cozy up on the couch for the weekend. But now I have to go through with this.

Fuck.

Suddenly realizing I'm standing in my dress, Pari springs to her feet. "*Way-ver-ly.* Are you fucking kidding me? You look stunning!"

That's the reaction I was hoping for. "Yeah?"

She motions with her finger for me to twirl, and even though I feel silly and vulnerable and a little obnoxious, I do it.

Pari grins from ear to ear. "You're gonna make Ash regret ditching you, that's for damn sure."

My heart skips a beat. In just a few short hours, I'll be in Ash's orbit again. Breathing the same air. Maybe by the end of the night, I'll be holding her hand. And if my dreams come true, kissing her.

I pace back and forth nervously while Pari gets dressed in my parents' room. There's no going back now. I'm really going to the Webber Academy ball. As Caroline. To see Ash.

God, I hope I can pull this off.

Interrupting my mind spin, Pari practically leaps out of the bedroom in her dress, a bright smile on her face. "Ta-da!"

"Whoa," I say with a gasp. "You look like a princess!"

She raises an eyebrow. "I think you mean a queen."

I bow before her. She really does look gorgeous. Her dress is white up top and subtly fades into gold at the bottom. Her long sleeves are woven with delicate lace, and she even has a brand-new cane.

"I've named her . . . Selma," she says as she holds it up. It's hammered gold, the tiny indents shimmering in the light. The handle hooks around so it's easy to hold, with a stunning floral engraving around it. "After Selma Blair, of course."

"She's beautiful," I say, marveling at it.

Pari grins as she struts over to her bag, pulls out her mask, and slips it over her eyes. Hers isn't a full face mask like Caroline's, but it's just as beautiful. It's white, with gold trim and feathers spread out like wings on either side. I tie the gold ribbon behind her head, letting it gently flow down with her long, dark hair.

Pari returns the favor, helping secure my mask. "Go bold or go home," she says again as the heavy gold mask completes my disguise.

I nod and remind myself to embrace this night just as Caroline would. I'm not a shy scholarship kid tonight. I'm Manhattan royalty. Tonight, I'm Cinder-fucking-ella.

CHAPTER FOUR

Y ou girls going to a party?" the Lyft driver asks as he pulls away from my block. Our dresses floof up to our chins in the tiny back seat.

"A ball!" Pari replies with the biggest grin. Her excitement is electric; it's amping up the butterflies in my stomach.

But then the ride into the city and downtown is bumpy, with so much stopping and starting that it doesn't take long for those butterflies to start spinning in circles and flying into each other. I can feel my anxiety expanding inside me like a balloon filling with water. The traffic around us is loud and bright and suddenly I can't think of anything but getting out of this car and running home.

And then . . .

"We're here."

Pari puts her hand on mine and I snap back to reality. "You good?"

I move to rub my hands on my thighs to dry the nervous sweat building up, but stop myself when I remember I'm wearing a dress that costs more than a year's rent for my parents. "Yep. Yep. Good. Yep."

I make sure my mask is secured and climb out of the car, then watch as it turns the corner. My feet want to run. Back the way we came. People on the street eye me curiously. What do they see? Do I look tense? Do I look like I belong in this dress? I loosen up my shoulders, and then take a step forward, and then another.

We arranged for the Lyft to drop me off a block away from the event so that no one would see "Caroline" arrive with Pari and start asking questions. I turn the corner to see a line of shiny luxury cars and wide Hummer limousines. Pari poses on the red carpet next to Frank, his legs a little too long for his tux, his mask apparently a little too loose on his face since he has to keep pushing it up. It's a simple white eye covering that looks like it came from a Spirit Halloween store, but it works.

More classmates step out onto the sidewalk, dressed to the nines. They all stop on the red carpet to be snapped by the hired paparazzi and take selfies, before they have to hand their phones in to security. I'm about to step onto the street when a car speeds past, tooting its horn so loudly that I jump out of my skin. I back way up and hide, pressing myself against the brick of the closest building, clutching my chest.

Can I just stay here all night? I'm freaking out. Time to whip out some of my anxiety-reducing tricks.

Breathe in for five. Out for five. Focus on my surroundings.

I stare up at the Webber Sewing Factory. Sitting proudly on the edge of the East River in the shadow of the Brooklyn Bridge, flanked by exclusive restaurants on cobblestone streets, the Sewing Factory looks like someone plucked it out of the nineteenth century and dropped it into modern downtown Manhattan. The old printed signage on the front is faded, but in a way that's come back in style, and the wide arched windows allow a view into the packed venue. It stands ten stories high and with multiple buildings connected by covered walkways, and according to Google Maps it even has helipads on the roof.

My heart rate returns to its normal anxious levels, so I straighten my shoulders, check for oncoming traffic, and then push myself ahead.

All eyes turn to me as I approach, and I forget how to breathe.

What would Caroline do? She'd probably put on a real show, as if she were on *Drag Race*. I'm not at that level, but I throw a couple of poses I've seen influencers use on Instagram a bazillion times. Claw hand on hips. One leg forward. Shoulders back. Or is it shoulders forward? God, this is uncomfortable. I feel like a pretzel.

Pari joins me and subtly coaches my poses, mouthing the words "Fucking relax!" Easier said than done, my friend. People are whispering around me. My auditory processing isn't the best, so I can't make out exactly what's being said, but I pick up "Caroline" and "father" and "brave," so it's enough to piece together what the topic of conversation will be tonight.

"I feel like we're at the Met Gala," I say to Pari, trying to focus on the glamour of it all.

"Honey." Pari blows me a kiss. "The Met Gala wishes!" She poses with her new gold cane, beaming with pride.

Photographers lean in to get photos of her as she struts off the red carpet and toward the doors.

The Brooklyn Bridge towers over us, the water below rippling in the evening breeze as we step closer to the main entrance: two arching double doors, decorated with spring flowers and string lights. A tall guard stands to either side. The security team all wear black suits, Taser guns attached to their hips, and matching masks that are both beautiful and chilling. They are stark white and Venetian with a long nose, and an angel cherub has been carved into the top, just above the eyes. I'm so busy staring at it that I almost screw up when one of the guards asks for my name.

"Wa—Caroline," I say. "Caroline Sinclair."

I try to act calm as he checks his list on the iPad in his hands, but my heart is pounding. He gives me another look, then nods.

Another guard greets us in the foyer. He's at least six feet tall, with wide shoulders and a Jason Statham vibe coming off of him. His mask is gold, and I assume he must be the head of Webber's security team. A name badge on his chest says MASON. My dad said something about Webber hiring a new security firm—this must be them.

"Phones" is all he says, his voice deep and no-nonsense. He gestures to a line of metal boxes on a marble table behind

him. I watch others ahead of me go through the process, so I
know what to do: check in our phone through a scanner on
the table, then place our phone in its own little baggie, which
then goes into one of the heavy-duty lockboxes.

Pari rolls her eyes. Frank and I dutifully scan our phones
and place them in their baggies and box, but Pari only pretends to. Instead, she waits for the guard to look away and
slides it down the front of her dress. She winks at me, and I
wink back. Maybe one day, I won't have to fake bravery.

I gasp as we pass through the heavy sliding doors into a
ballroom so grand Gatsby would envy it. The red brick walls
glow against thousands of twinkling lights dangling from the
ceiling like stars in a night sky. People mingling on the mezzanine above could reach out and touch them, but they're all
too interested in watching the dance floor down below. Heels
clip against the refurbished hardwood; dotted around the edge
are Moroccan-style carpets under leather couches and winged
armchairs, for those who want a break from dancing. The entire wall behind the stage is covered in ivy, and an arch of metallic gold balloons reaches over the DJ booth and booming
main speakers.

The Webber Sewing Factory used to be just that. Back
in the early 1900s, the Webber family found their fortune in
garment manufacturing, and this was where it all began. It's
no longer a factory, of course, having been converted into an
event space for sleek celebrity weddings and corporate functions for the Big Five in tech and media. And let's not forget
the extravagant fundraisers Dean Webber holds multiple times

a year. The Webber Academy campus may be his crown jewel, but this factory is his family's legacy. This is where he honors the newest member of the Dean's Society, like he'll do tonight.

Waiters in white tuxes circle the room carrying golden trays, holding what appear to be cocktail glasses filled with green juice and kombucha—very on-brand for Dean Webber, who is obsessed with what he calls "optimized living." It's the same kind of clean-eating stuff he insists my mom and the other school chefs provide for us in the student cafés.

My classmates gather together in groups while their parents mingle and catch up with younger children clutching their legs or running around wildly. I haven't even been here five minutes before people start talking to me like I'm Caroline.

"Hey, how's your dad?" Lance asks.

"Uh, um," I stutter. I reach for one of the answers I've prepped in my mind—scripting conversations ahead of time is a helpful tool I've learned to navigate stressful social situations. "He's hanging in there."

Lance gives me a sad nod. I turn to walk away before he can ask me anything else, but his parents are waiting with pasted-on smiles, both their heads tilted slightly to the right, hands clasped in front of them. Mr. Howard is wearing a mask that covers the top half of his face, with short stag-like horns reaching out from the top. I've only seen him around campus a few times, but he comes off as arrogant and entitled, and refers to himself as the New Wolf of Wall Street. Mrs. Howard's mask is more like a deer, delicate and feminine. Her dress is midnight black, covering every inch of skin from her neck to the tips of her fingers. They both reach out for me, and I instinctively step back. Something about the look in their eyes feels predatory.

"Aww," Mrs. Howard says. "We didn't mean to startle you, darling. Our hearts are just so broken for you."

They each take one of my hands and squeeze until my knuckles shift painfully under my skin.

"Your father will be so proud of you," Mr. Howard says. "For the way you're putting the family first like this. I'm sure you will be greatly rewarded."

"O . . . kay." I'm glad they can't see my face under this mask, because I'm not sure I could hide how creeped out I am.

That's when I see her. Ash. Behind the Howards, on the other side of the floor. She's glowing in a blush-pink A-line gown that sits perfectly off her shoulders. Her honey-brown hair is styled into a short, wavy bob, and her bejeweled mask sparkles under the lights. It only covers the top half of her face. My breath catches in my throat at the sight of her.

"Thank you," I say to Lance's parents. Then I slowly pry my hands out of their iron grips. "If you'll excuse me." I curtsy, which is weird, but I don't know how to act around rich people.

Mrs. Howard gives me a sympathetic smile. "Of course, dear. Enjoy the night, and we'll see you for the after-party." She winks as she says "after-party," and I just nod and walk away. I shake off the weirdness and train my gaze back on Ash.

It takes all my restraint to stop myself from dashing through the crowd and into her arms. But I have to be smart about this. Be cool. Chill. Can't let myself be the lovesick ex-girlfriend, at least not until I know she misses me as much as I miss her.

Besides, even if running to her wouldn't look desperate, it's still a bad idea—I'm supposed to be Caroline. Plus, Ash's dad is standing right next to her. They're smiling and talking at the corner by the stage, surrounded by a handful of men in tuxedos. Dean Webber's mask is black and gold with horns, kind of like a minotaur. The men around them have similar masks, but their horns are smaller, like Brett Howard's mask. I try not to wonder too much if the horn sizes represent some kind of phallic chain of command, because gross. I can't see their full faces, but I can bet they are the same circle of men who follow Webber around wherever he goes.

There's Dr. Bradley, Jack's dad. Congressman George, Alice's dad, is always in Webber's ear about something. And then there's Brett, Lance's dad, who saunters over and slaps Webber on the back. The oldest in their group is Sheldon Morrison, the New York City police commissioner and an old friend of the late Owen Webber, Sr. The youngest member of their Frat Pack is Jeff Ramsey, the founder of a huge social media company, whose kid just started at Webber Elementary.

I only know all these names because my parents have mentioned them. Apparently, they're always having late-night meetings in Webber's office, getting drunk on cognac and making a mess that my dad has to clean up the next morning. Normally, Caroline's dad would be right there with them. Instead he's fighting for his life, and his closest friends are all right here, drinking expensive champagne and laughing like they don't have a care in the world.

I guess money really doesn't buy everything.

Ash tries to leave the circle of minotaur-masked men, but her dad subtly holds her arm while talking with his buddies. He's no doubt bragging about his daughter to all his high-powered pals, showing her off as the poster child for an education only Webber Academy can provide. She loathes when he does that. I can practically see her cheeks flushing red from embarrassment from the other side of the room.

That urge to run over to her only grows stronger. I settle for staring at her like a creep instead.

As though sensing my gaze, she glances my way, and our eyes lock. A jolt of electricity shoots up my spine. But then she looks away, like she's totally unaffected, and I remember she can't see my face. I'm Caroline tonight, not Waverly.

"Oh my god!" Pari squeals next to me, clutching my hand. "I love this song!" I've been so immersed in Ash that I haven't been paying attention to anything else. "Let's dance!"

Pari and Frank start heading for the floor, but I hang back. "I'll meet you out there."

They shrug and push their way into the middle, then start moving to the beat. My senses feel like they are under attack from a wild riot of lights, sounds, and motion all around me. I fidget with the earplugs in my ears, then cover them up with my hair again, letting it drape over my shoulders.

I watch closely as Dean Webber leads his horned friends upstairs to what I can only assume is some kind of private

Old White Man Lounge where they can discuss the stock market or new boat purchases or whatever it is rich parents talk about. I take the opportunity to start walking toward Ash when a girl in a bright yellow dress grabs me by the wrist and whisks me into a side room.

"Caroline," the girl says. "You're here. Thank *god*."

It takes me a second to recognize who it is, but when I see her stare down the other three people in the room until they leave, I tense. Only one girl has that kind of terrifying power over the student body—Max.

Once we're alone, she pulls me into a tight hug, then holds me at arm's length so she can look at me. "God, poor you. Poor Gregory! How's he doing?"

Out of guilt and fear that my voice will give me away, I don't say anything. Max frowns, genuine hurt in her eyes.

"If there's anything I can do," she says softly. "You know I'm here, right?"

I nod, and that seems to placate her a little.

Max is gorgeous tonight. Her dark brown skin shimmers with what must be highlighter and body glitter, making her look like she's glowing from the inside out. Her mask is made from yellow flower petals that match her ruffled dress. Her tight curls fall onto her shoulders, sparkling like her skin.

She opens her mouth to say something, but then closes it again.

"What?" I say before I can stop myself, my curiosity getting the better of me.

"Okay," she says to me in a hushed tone. "I have to tell you something. It's about Jack. But I understand if you don't want to hear it."

I lean in, any nerves I felt about being alone with her disappearing at the prospect of hearing gossip about my least favorite person. Besides, I owe it to Caroline to find out if he's cheating. At least I can do a little reconnaissance on her behalf. "What is it?"

But before she can tell me more, who should walk in but Mr. Boat Shoes himself.

Jack Bradley, Caroline's sometime boyfriend, and son of Dr. Bradley, aka the boy heir to Cobalt Pharmaceuticals, the same company that upped the price of my mother's MS meds out of pure greed, so the Bradleys could buy another yacht for Jack to post all over Instagram.

"Look!" Jack calls from the doorway, pointing to me with a wobbly finger. "My girl made it after all!"

Jack's mask is white with three faces, one in front and on either side. It gives me the creeps. His bow tie is also askew, and even from five feet away, I can smell the bourbon on him.

Max positions herself in front of me defensively. "Do you mind? We're talking."

"'Do you mind?'" Jack mimics her.

He stumbles over to me and takes my hand, pulling me back into the ballroom and onto the dance floor. My nervous stomach doesn't appreciate my being dragged around like a doll, and it only gets worse when he puts his hands on my waist and starts pressing himself against me. I fight the urge to recoil and run, knowing that it would only make people suspicious, but even if I were straight, this would just be gross.

Caroline said that she's mad at him, so I could use that, do some method acting, start a fight to get away from him—but Jack isn't exactly an even-tempered guy. What if he yells? Or causes a huge scene? I can't handle that kind of aggression. Caroline never backs down from a fight, but when a situation gets too heavy for me, my usual reaction is to run and hide somewhere I can stim quietly until I feel okay again. Looking around the grand ballroom, I'm pretty sure there aren't any sensory rooms tucked away for people like me.

The safest option is to placate Jack until I can find a believable reason to get away from him. I hate to admit it, but he scares the hell out of me.

"You seem shorter," he says, looking down at my dress. "Are you wearing different heels?"

Shit. Damn my slouchy spine. I shake my head and try to straighten my back a little more, stand a little taller, but that only makes him narrow his eyes at me. I look everywhere but at him, trying to find an escape route.

That's when I see Ash again. She's sitting in an armchair, watching us intently. Does she recognize me? Can she see the little freckles on my shoulders, the ones she'd kiss so sweetly when we were supposed to be studying? No, she's too far away. But if anyone could spot me in this getup, it'd be Ash. No one knows my body better than she does.

She finally breaks our gaze when Jack spins us around the

floor. But I can't help it, I keep stealing glances at her from across the room.

"Hey," Jack says into my ear.

I look at him and he nods toward Ash. "You're supposed to be *my* girlfriend, remember?"

Wait, does Jack know I'm not Caroline? Maybe he's not as oblivious as Caroline thought. I need to smarten up. There's too much at stake for me to get busted, especially before I can even do what I came here to do.

What would Caroline say?

"You're the one who keeps ghosting me." I do my best impression of her.

He laughs under his mask, then pulls me closer, sliding a hand down past my hip. I grit my teeth.

As I'm uncomfortably squished against Jack, I catch sight of Pari and Frank dancing a few feet away. I stare at them like a Jedi trying to mind-control them into looking my way, hoping they'll save me, but they're having way too much fun to notice.

The song ends, and Jack pulls away to bow like an actual gentleman . . . only to stumble into someone and cause them to spill kombucha all over themselves. He ignores their hurled insults and looks back at me, grinning. "Shall we have another dance?"

Over his shoulder, I spot Ash hurrying up the staircase to the mezzanine.

"Um, maybe later?"

Then I hike up my dress and head for the stairs.

CHAPTER FIVE

F riggin' perfect," my dad grumbles as we step out of our building. I follow his line of sight to see his car covered in a thick pile of snow and ice. "Hon, go back inside and wait while Waves and I take care of this."

"I can help," Mom says.

"Don't argue with me on this," Dad says quietly but sternly. Mom turns and goes back inside. The cold aggravates her joint pain, so it's better for her to wait inside, but Dad is pissed at me, so it's better for me if she stays out here as a buffer.

"I'll start the car and get it defrosted," he says without looking at me. "You start shoving the snow off the top."

I nod and get to work. He's mad because I took so long finding my scarf this morning. I have a habit of putting things down and then forgetting about them, especially when I get home from school and just throw everything off of me. My scarf ended up being under a pile of library books by the front door, but I looked everywhere else before finding it there, and now we're approximately fifteen minutes behind our morning schedule, and we're all on edge. I knew Dad was pissed when he suggested I just take one of Mom's scarves, and he knew I was pissed when I snapped at him that Mom's scarves aren't part of the Webber uniform.

So now we're both in a mood, running late and freezing cold as we try to get our old car out of a blanket of snow.

When it's finally free, my dad waves my mom out, we all hop in the car, and in one more cruel joke by the universe, the engine refuses to start. My dad swears. I drop my head back against the car seat in defeat. My mom laughs.

"Sorry," she says. "I know it's not funny. But it is a little funny."

Dad and I sneak a smile at each other, and just like that, Mom has lightened our dark moods.

"Okay," Dad says. "We have two options. We can sit here and try to will this damn car to life, or we cut our losses and head for the subway. Either way we're gonna be late."

Mom pats his leg. "Let's just take the subway."

We half walk, half run to the subway station, but when we get to the entrance Mom slips on ice and suddenly she's falling down the stairs, her back slamming into the edges of the concrete steps.

"Mom!" I yell. Dad and I rush down to her while other people try to help her up.

"I'm fine," she says, waving everyone off. But her voice is strained, and tears well in her eyes.

Dad hands me his phone. "Call a Lyft." Then, in a feat of strength I've never ever seen from my dad, he scoops my mom up in his arms and carries her up the stairs and back onto the street.

I order a Lyft car to take us to the nearest urgent care center. The car pulls up and my dad helps my mom in, and just as I'm about to get in, too, he stops me.

"You're going to school."

"What? No way! I'm going with you guys."

He shakes his head. "Waverly, you can't miss a day. You have a scholarship to think of. Your mom will be fine. I'll keep you updated the whole time."

"Dad—"

"You've got your earplugs for the train?"

I nod, pouting.

"Good. Now, hurry. Get to school. Love you, kid."

I turn and head down to the subway, shoving the earplugs in with shaking fingers. My mind replays the sight of my mom falling, then creates terrible scenarios of what might happen to her at urgent care. I spend the whole train ride into the city crying.

If I weren't so disorganized, if I had just put my scarf in my bag or hung it up with my school blazer when I got home from school the day before, we would've had more time to deal with the car, we wouldn't have had to run to the subway, and my mom never would have fallen. This is all my fault.

By the time I make it in to school, I've missed first period and I'm being mercilessly strangled by anxiety. I spend another thirty minutes waiting outside Webber's office for a late pass while he finishes up a call, but it gives me time to splash my face in the bathroom and try to get my shit together. I don't want him to know how much of a mess I am this morning.

"Waverly!" he says with a wide, toothy grin when I walk into his office. Light pours in from the tall arched windows, making him glow. "Take a seat! How are you? How are your parents?"

"Fine," I croak. My bottom lip quivers like a little bitch's. I pretend to scratch my nose in an attempt to hide it, but it's no use.

"Waverly," he says, leaning over his desk. His eyes pierce mine. "Is everything okay?"

I shake my head, and then it all comes tumbling out of me. I tell him about my terrible morning, the scarf, the snow-covered car, Mom falling down the steps, how she's at urgent care right now and I don't know if she's okay or not.

"I'm really sorry for being late," I say between sobs. "I know attendance counts toward my scholarship evaluation, but I—"

"What hospital did they go to?" he asks as he picks up the phone on his desk.

I check my texts for updates from my dad. "Elmhurst, in Queens."

"Laura," he says into the receiver, talking to his secretary.

I sit across from his desk in stunned silence as he organizes a private room in Mount Sinai Hospital on the Upper East

Side and specifically requests the best specialists in the city to meet them there.

Panic clutches my chest. "No, no. We can't afford that!"

Mr. Webber holds a palm up. "I'll take care of it. You're family."

Oh, no. I'm gonna cry again. I mumble a thank-you and something about getting to class, then stand up to leave. And walk right into Ashley Webber, the dean's perfect daughter, who just walked into his office.

The stack of papers she was holding falls to the floor. My slow reflexes and brain fog render me useless for a moment, and I just stand there watching her fumble to pick it all up.

"Sorry, sorry," I say when I finally join her on the hardwood floor, helping her gather the last few pieces. It's her college applications; Harvard, Yale, Oxford. Impressive titles. I'm sure she'll get into all of them.

"It's my fault," Ash says. "I should have knocked. I didn't know anyone else was in here."

We both stand up, and I straighten my skirt, trying to look like I'm okay.

Webber covers the phone with his palm to say, "Waverly, do you know my daughter, Ashley?"

I almost say no. I almost pretend not to know her even though we sit in the same AP Biology class. She sits in the back with her friends; there's no way she knows who I am.

"Oh, yes! We take AP Bio together," she says.

My mouth falls open. "Yeah. Right."

Webber nods to the papers in Ashley's hand. "Is that it?"

"Yes," she says, then says to me, "I've been asked to write an essay on why I should take a year off before college to travel." She rolls her eyes, and I laugh like I can totally relate.

"Very good," Webber says before adding the essay to a pile on his desk. Then his smile returns. "Ashley, honey, I need you to do something for me. Could you accompany Waverly to Mount Sinai?"

Ashley nods. "Of course. Is everything okay?"

"Uh," I start. "My mom had a fall. But I really should be getting to class. I've already missed—"

Webber wags a finger to silence me. "Nonsense. Family comes first, that's what I always say. Ashley will make sure you get to the hospital safely so you can be with your parents. Tell them not to worry about making up their shifts. They'll be paid for today and the rest of the week while your mother gets the rest she needs."

I don't say anything. I can't. I've never experienced such generosity in my life. I thank him repeatedly and leave with Ashley, taking their town car to the hospital.

For six hours, Ashley sits with me in the busy waiting area while televisions blare with competing cable news broadcasts and people rush in and out around us. Dad checks in on me every now and then to tell me they're still waiting, that Mom's doing fine. The bags under his eyes grow darker with each passing hour, but I pretend not to notice.

I tell Ashley all about my mom's chronic pain, and she listens like no one has ever listened to me before. I feel exposed and vulnerable and seen and valid all at the same time.

"She's just always sore," I try to explain, but it's hard when I haven't experienced it myself. "Mom says it's like waking up after being hit by a bus, only it's every day."

"That sounds awful," Ashley says with a frown. "And no doctors have diagnosed it?"

"Nope." The bitterness in my voice is thick. "Not that they've tried that hard. Mostly they tell her to lose weight, or get more sleep. No one listened, so she stopped trying."

"Fuck them."

Whoa. I've never heard Ashley Webber swear before. It's kind of hot. I turn to her, and notice the fierceness in her eyes, the tension in her jaw.

"Seriously," she says. "So many people are ignored when they need help. You should see the statistics, especially for Black and brown women. It's disgusting how many get turned away when they need lifesaving care."

Uh-oh, she's turned the conversation onto my special interest. If I start talking about this, I won't be able to stop, and in the past my monologuing has been known to annoy people.

"Mm-hmm." I hold it all in. All the facts I want to spew out, the studies I want to cite, the career I have planned for myself to tackle all of it. I swallow it down. I want her to like me.

"My mom worked in medicine, you know?" she says softly. "She ran her own clinic focusing on women's health and did some work with Planned Parenthood, too."

Wow, her mom was cool. I nod, because I'm still holding in my monologue.

"I want to do that, too," she continues. "I like to think that if I was the doctor your mom went to for help, I would have listened. It wouldn't have to take someone like my dad using his money and connections, calling in expensive specialists to get her heard. That's something my dad doesn't get; he thinks he's gaming the system by hooking your mom up with these doctors, but really he's just another player in it. He *is* the system."

I don't know why, but I feel a pinch of defensiveness rise up inside me. "Maybe the only way to game the system is to play it first?" It comes out as a question because let's be real, I don't know what I'm talking about. "But for what it's worth, I'm so grateful to your dad. He's done so much for me and my parents, we'll never be able to repay him. Because of him and the school he's built, I'll be able to go to a great college and work in medicine, too. Who knows, maybe you and me will end up working together one day!"

She smiles. "You're going into medicine, too?"

Boom. Monologue activated. I tell her all about my big dreams of being a doctor and how I'm going to change the system from the inside and that I think her mom was super cool for working with PP. Not only does Ashley not get annoyed at my rambling, breathless run-on sentence, she listens eagerly, nods along, and smiles.

Once I've let it all out, I take in a breath, and force myself to change the subject. "So, does your dad always make you write essays when you want something?"

She sighs. "Whenever I want something that my dad doesn't agree with, yeah. He asks me to write a two-thousand-word essay explaining why I want to do it, the benefits, and how it will affect my future."

"Wow," I said. "That sounds . . . intense."

She laughs. "I hate it with a passion, but it's the only way I can get him to see my side of things. I had to write an essay explaining why I wanted a puppy when I was ten. He still wouldn't let me get one, though, so it doesn't always work."

"And this essay was about taking a year off before college?"

"My mom loved to travel," she explains. "When I was little, she'd tell me stories about her trips to Paris and Milan and London. We'd go through old photo albums from her adventures through Europe. She'd talk about the places she'd stayed, the people she'd met. I wanted that. As a family, we'd planned for us to spend a few months traveling once I graduated high school. But my dad doesn't want to do it anymore. I'm hoping my essay will convince him to at least *let me go*."

She emphasizes the words "let me go" and clenches her fists together as she says it. I get the impression that he's become overly protective of her since her mother died.

We talk about school, college preferences, movies, books. We bond over our favorite queer YA contemporary romance books, our shared love of Zendaya, I tell her about my cats, and in these conversations we come out to each other in a hundred tiny ways.

It never occurred to me that Ashley could be gay. She's supposed to be the dean's perfect, straight-A daughter—emphasis on straight. But then again, since when does perfect equal straight? Hello there, internalized homophobia.

I've been out at school since day one, and so has Pari. There aren't a ton of openly queer students at Webber, but those of us who are out know about one another. We nod at one another in the halls, like one another's astrology memes on Instagram, and support one another in the fight against the oppressive straight culture of our peers. Okay, maybe that last one is a little dramatic, but still. Ashley never even gave us a sideways glance in the hall, and her Instagram was sparce aside from a few photos of her playing tennis. Didn't scream sapphic to me at all, but I was wrong.

"Can I confess something to you?" I ask, my gaze planted firmly on the cold coffee cup in my hands.

"Sure."

"I was surprised this morning," I say, "when you remembered me from bio. I didn't think you had ever noticed me."

I sneak a glance at her, and she's staring at her own coffee cup.

She smirks, and her cheeks flush as pink as her lips. "I've noticed you."

I feel giddy. "I've noticed you, too." The words tumble out of my mouth clumsily, but she hears me. She reaches out and takes my hand in hers, and suddenly the drab, anxiety-riddled waiting room becomes the most romantic place in the world. Even the fluorescent lighting and crushing sensory overload feel a little easier. We sit like that, hand in hand, until my dad comes over to update me on my mom.

"They're doing all the tests." He rubs his hand through his hair, and he looks like he hasn't slept in weeks. "All the tests she's been asking for for years."

"That's great!" I clap with excitement. "How's she feeling? Is her back okay? How are you?"

He falls into a seat next to me. "They put her on some pain meds so she's kinda out of it, but she's not in pain anymore. They did X-rays and her back is bruised, but there's no serious damage from the fall. But listen, honey, we're gonna be here awhile. You should go home and get some rest."

Go home? By myself? Anxiety flashes go through my mind: the subway in rush hour; eating cheese and Ritz for dinner alone; going to bed knowing my parents are still at the hospital; waking up tomorrow all by myself. That's too much for me to process when I'm already running on a low battery from today's chaos.

"Waverly can sleep at my house," Ashley says.

A whole new series of anxiety flashes race through my mind: I don't have any of my clothes; I'll be completely out of my comfort zone; what if they eat weird rich-people food that I don't like?

But at least there, I wouldn't be alone. I'd be with Ashley. And right now, she's kind of the only person I want to be with.

"Is that okay with you?" Dad looks at me, and I can tell by the doubt in his eyes that he's fully expecting me to say no. He knows I hate unexpected changes like this. But he doesn't know how cool Ashley Webber is.

"Yes," I say.

Dad smiles. "Okay. Thank you, Ashley. And tell your father thank you, too. We owe you guys the world."

Ashley shrugs. "It's like he always says, we're family."

. . .

"I can't believe I've never seen this movie," Ashley says. We're sitting in her theater room—yes, an actual theater room with twelve cinema-style chairs and a big screen—eating pizza. Her dad isn't home; apparently he always works late, which seems kinda lonely for Ashley.

We're watching *The Mitchells vs. the Machines,* my go-to comfort movie for when I've had a bad day. But I can't focus. She's sitting super close to me, like, closer than she needs to considering there are ten other chairs in this room. The pizza box sits open on top of our laps, and every time she reaches for another slice I flinch. Then she side-eyes me, I pretend not to see her side-eyeing me, my cheeks burn, and I start sweating so hard I'm worried about leaving wet patches on the chair.

"The Mitchells are totally all autistic," I say. "Or neurodivergent in some way. That's why I love this so much."

"And also the pug is adorable," she says.

"That, too," I say, laughing.

There's a heavy pause, and then she says, "I don't know if I should say this, but today has been really great."

My whole body tingles. "Why shouldn't you say that?"

"Because your mom is in the hospital, Waverly."

"Oh." Of course. "Yeah. Today started out as the worst day ever for me. But thanks to your dad, she's getting more help than she's ever had access to. We might find out what's been causing all her pain, and then they'll be able to treat it. This is good. This is a good day, Ashley."

"You can call me Ash, you know," she says with a small smile. "My friends call me Ash. My dad calls me Ashley."

"Oh, okay." I feel like I've been given a key into a new world. "Ash."

She sighs. "You know what I'd be doing if you weren't here?"

I shrug.

"I'd be getting home from my tennis lesson." She rolls her eyes. "I hate tennis. Thousands of dollars on lessons and I'm still terrible at it. But you know what parents are like, right? Every hour has to be scheduled for some extracurricular activity. Not a minute wasted."

I nod, but my mom and dad aren't like the other parents at Webber Academy at all—and I don't just mean income levels. Webber moms all wear Lululemon athleisure gear, all the time, while my mom is either in her chef's uniform or in her best Old Navy dresses. My mom stays on campus to work in the kitchen while the other moms go to meet with their personal trainers or to their SoulCycle classes—but they always come back to meet with their kids' advisors and teachers to discuss homework or grades they want changed.

And don't get me started on the dads. They hang out in groups, looking like an episode of *Succession,* talking about stock prices or what the Webber Academy basketball team needs to do to win the championship.

At my old school, parents didn't have time to hang out in the hallways of their kids' school, stalking teachers they don't like or dropping off projects they absolutely did for their child. Public school parents had jobs that didn't give them that kind of freedom, sometimes two jobs, and no au pairs or housekeepers or drivers or tutors to help.

"What's your schedule like for tomorrow?" I ask her.

Ash leans her head back on the chair. "I have to wake up at five forty-five because my personal trainer arrives at six. We work out for an hour, then I shower, eat, go to school. After school I have to meet with my academic advisor to talk about college applications again. Then I have a violin lesson. Oh, and a dress fitting for a charity auction my dad is dragging me to next week. Hopefully I'll make it home by nine to get my homework done."

I stare at her, mouth hanging open, and she laughs.

"Why are you looking at me like that?" she asks.

All I know is if that were my daily schedule, I'd have to add some room in my calendar for a weekly emotional breakdown, because that is one hundred percent too much.

"I know there are a lot of overachievers at our school, but wow," I say.

Ash looks wounded, and I worry I said the wrong thing. She smiles, but it doesn't reach her eyes. "When you're the daughter of the king, you have to prove you're worthy of the throne."

"So, no pressure, then," I say, and that makes her laugh in a way that fills the room. "Well, if you ever need a break from the micromanaging"—I place my hand on my chest—"I happen to be a sought-after tutor. Your dad would think we're studying, but instead we could just be numbing our brains with social media and destroying our teeth with candy."

She laughs even louder then, and I beam with pride for having caused that kind of joy.

"You know," she says. "I might take you up on that."

Ash leans in. She reaches her hand up and pushes a strand of hair behind my ear. I'm frozen. I have no idea what happened to cause this sudden turn of events. The mood in the room has softened. She tries to keep eye contact with me, and god I try to match her intensity but I just can't. I look down at my hands, and she takes them in hers. Her thumb strokes the skin of my palm, and I feel it all the way down my back.

She leans in closer, and I tilt my head back up and close my eyes. Her lips touch mine. My fingers start to shake from nerves, so she holds them tighter. Then kisses me harder. The movie must end, because we're sitting in darkness, in silence, just us, making out in an empty theater room. I've imagined my first kiss so many times, so many ways, but none of those fantasies included Ash Webber. Never in my wildest dreams did I think I'd get to kiss her.

CHAPTER SIX

NOW

The mezzanine is even busier than the main floor. This is where most of the adults have gathered, letting the students take the dance floor downstairs. Along with parents are staff and faculty from school, and it's super weird to see teachers all glitzed and glammed and downing cocktails like they're unsupervised kids at a party. They perch elegantly on velvet couches pressed along the walls and crowd around one another under the low-lit chandeliers. Deep red walls with gold metallic accents add a Victorian twist that reminds me of horror movies about haunted houses. And right now, Ash is the ghost I'm chasing through the halls.

I catch a glimpse of her rounding a corner and twist my way through the moving bodies. Random hands pat my shoulder as I hurry past, with sympathetic platitudes about Caroline's dad.

"So brave of you to come," Mrs. Mathis, the school nurse, says.

"Your father is in all our thoughts," Mr. Cameron adds.

I don't know how to respond, so I nod and keep going. I'm not in the mood to be touched by people, and my skin itches from where their hands made contact. What's worse, hearing all these kindnesses makes me feel like a terrible person. I'm pretending to be my distressed friend just to see the girl who broke my heart. Is this who I am now? Maybe I'm no better than Jack and his drug-peddling, price-hiking father: using others to get what I want, no matter the cost.

Before I can sink even further into my shame spiral, I see her.

She's standing in an alcove, silhouetted by the purple sky through a tall arched window. And she's not alone.

A brunette in an emerald-green dress stands close to her, inches from her face. She's wearing a black mask with gold cracks running through it. I can't hear what they're saying, but I can tell from Ash's demeanor that she's tense. She's always hated confrontation, and this mystery girl in green seems mad as hell. Like, fists-clenched, feet-stomping, Karen-about-to-ask-for-the-manager mad as hell.

Ash nods her head, and the girl grabs her by the shoulders and actually shakes her. I step forward, ready to defend Ash, to knock the other girl's hands away. But I stop myself. It's not my place. Not anymore. Then I wonder . . . The passion in this interaction, the way they're arguing, it's clear they know each other. Am I witnessing a couple's spat?

The thought makes my stomach turn, and I sidle behind a tall vase of flowers, out of view. How did I not think of this before? Of course Ash would have moved on and found someone else. She's probably dating some British heiress, one of Princes Harry and William's lesser-known but just as royal cousins. I feel like the biggest fool on the planet. Suddenly this damn dress feels ridiculous and much too tight. I need to get out of here. I need air.

I turn on my heels and run back the way I came, back through the crowded mezzanine filled with sympathy land mines, back down the stairs into the main ballroom. Just as I'm about to reach the double doors to the glorious outside world, a spotlight lands on me.

"Excuse me," a voice booms from above.

I freeze like the Weeping Angels in *Doctor Who.* My skin prickles. I've been busted.

But then, the light swivels off me as quickly as it landed, moving over the crowded dance floor with a handful of other colorful lights. Everyone turns to face the stage, and I do the same, my heartbeat drumming in my ears from the close call.

"Good evening, ladies and gentlemen," Dean Webber says from the stage. He's standing comfortably in a tuxedo that fits him like a second skin, straight-shouldered and patient as he waits for all of us to quiet down.

"Thank you for coming out tonight," he continues. "You all look absolutely marvelous! You have truly outdone yourselves this year." He throws his arms out beside him. "Welcome to the Tenth Annual Webber Academy Masquerade!"

Everyone bursts into cheers and applause. I notice Ash hurrying down the stairs and toward the stage. The girl in the green dress is nowhere to be seen.

"Tonight is truly something special. I can't tell you how proud I am to see so many Webber Academy families here, all under one roof. Esteemed students, this magnificent ballroom—that I designed myself—is where you'll be tonight. Parents, I know you all need a night off to reap the benefits of your generous contributions to our community. There are many different VIP areas created just for you tonight. Building B has been transformed into the parents' wing. For the husbands, we have a grand cigar room, our bar complete with billiards and chess tables, and a cheeky little bowling alley. For the wives, we have provided a parlor for all your beauty needs—not that any of you need it, mind you!"

Some of the mothers laugh. I roll my eyes. What a bunch of heteronormative headassery. I'm surprised Dean Webber would buy into that, he's usually so progressive. Webber doesn't have any out trans students, but he still made the bathrooms gender neutral—and didn't back down when a few of the parents complained. At Webber, classroom windows are decorated with rainbows every Pride Month. He didn't flinch when I told him I was gay during the scholarship admissions interview. But gendered rooms for the husbands and wives? He must have succumbed to pressure from his more conservative donors or something.

"And there's also a bar especially for you ladies," the dean goes on. "With a wonderful library and indoor garden for you to stop and smell the roses. Before we start the celebrations, though, I'll be leading the adults through an interactive experience that will blow. Your. Mind.

"Adults only, sorry, students!"

Wow. He really hasn't spared a cent on this one-night gala. Couldn't that money have gone to the actual cause this ball is fundraising for? The gendered sections could have been cut and that cash could have probably added another two scholarships. "I know we are all so attached to our tech," he adds, a more serious tone in his voice. "But tonight, I wanted to introduce you to a new way of being. Or, rather, an old way of being that we as a society have lost sight of. One without social media or Google or twenty-four-hour news cycles. One that allows us to truly be with each other, to be in the moment and harken back to the good old days where everything was slower, simpler, sweeter."

Parents in the crowd nod and clap.

Ash stands by the stage, in the shadows. It's too dark to see her face, but I recognize her from the way she holds herself. One arm reaching across her torso to grip the other, where her fingertips are probably circling her elbow. That's what she does when she's nervous.

That's what she'd do when we'd be lying in bed together, her mind wandering. Only I was between her arms then, and it was my elbow she was caressing.

Now, as I watch her wait by the stage, I wonder if coming here was a fool's errand. After all this time, all the heartbreak, I'm still here, on standby. Waiting for her to come back to me.

"I have a final announcement to make," he says. "As some of you may have already noticed, my daughter Ashley has graced us with her presence this evening. I'm incredibly proud of how hard she has worked at Oxford this year. She has devoted herself to the world of medical science, following in the footsteps of her mother." He turns to Ash. "I wish she were here to see the adult you are becoming. She would be so proud of you."

Members of the audience clutch their hearts and sigh. Everyone knows that Mrs. Webber died of an aneurysm when Ash was a child. It feels good to see Ash stand a little taller after hearing that from her dad. His approval is one of the things Ash values most.

"So, family"—the dean clears his throat, wipes a stray tear from his eye—"it is my honor and privilege to introduce you to the Dean's Society's new student–alumni liaison. In the world to come, we will need leaders like my daughter. Come and join me, Ashley."

We all clap as she lifts her dress and walks up the steps to the stage. She adjusts her mask nervously and stands in front of the microphone.

"Thank you, Father," she says.

My heart perks up at the sound of her voice filling the room. God, I missed it. "And thank you, Webber Academy family. I'm honored to be trusted with this role."

As Ash is speaking, I hear Jack whispering Caroline's name from behind me. Pretending I don't hear him, I ease forward through the audience, moving closer to the stage and away from him. Maybe it's silly, but I hope if I can get close enough to Ash, she'll recognize it's me under this mask, and maybe, just maybe, that will mean something to her. Just like she still means something to me.

"I'm grateful and humbled," she continues, "to be chosen to help lead us into a new world."

That's weird. Her dad is always talking about building a new world, about preparing for the future, and Ash would always roll her eyes at it. Hearing her repeat the same words she used to laugh at hits me in an uncomfortable way, but I can't put my finger on why.

I reach the front of the crowd, quietly praying that she'll glance down and see me. Really see me.

"It feels so good to be back in New York," she says.

Cheers break out. She blushes and looks down, and that's when it happens. Our eyes lock. I give her the tiniest of waves, and she pauses, then smiles at me.

"Being away from you"—I swear she's talking directly to me—"from this place, was the hardest thing I've ever had to do. I left a big part of me here. I've missed you more than words can describe."

A chorus of "Aww" and "We missed you, too!" rings out. Meanwhile, my heart is trying to crash through my chest and into hers.

"I admit, I was hesitant to accept this role when my father offered it to me. I wanted to know that I'd earned it, that it wasn't just handed to me. I've worked hard since I left New York. I've learned what it means to sacrifice things for the greater good."

Oh, god. Does she mean me? She means me. I know it.

"I know nothing can really prepare us for what's to come," Ash says gravely. "But I trust that we will go forward together, as a family, just like my father has always said." She pauses to look out over the crowd, and sighs. "This probably doesn't make much sense right now, but I promise it will very soon. Until then, let's enjoy this incredible party my dad has organized just for us. A round of applause for my father!"

She closes her speech and the ballroom fills with applause. Something pulls me toward her, and I find myself at the base of the stage steps as she's walking down them. She trips on her dress, and I reach an arm out to catch her hand just as she steadies herself. Sparks jolt through my entire body as her hand takes mine. It's been so long since we've touched, but in this moment it feels like we never let go of each other.

Her eyes meet mine, and I swear I see a flash of recognition. This is my chance. I open my mouth to say something, but nothing comes out.

"Thank you," she says with a small smile.

"I've got you," I say.

It's like no time has passed. No hearts have been broken. No messages left on read. Her smile grows wider, her eyes searching mine behind the mask. I'm afraid to blink in case she disappears again. I want to take her away from here, go somewhere quiet, where we can be alone. There are so many things I've wanted to say to her for so long, things I need her to say to me. I need to know why she left me behind.

She opens her mouth to say something, but then her gaze

flickers over my shoulder, her smile vanishes, and I feel a large, sweaty hand on my lower back.

"Found you, babe," Jack says into my ear, making me flinch. His words drip like greasy oil on my skin.

Ash's hand slips out of mine, and a surge of anger runs through me. I glare at Jack, but it only makes him laugh. He drapes an arm around my shoulders, his damp armpit resting on my skin, making me want to puke.

Ash looks at me, then at him, and back at me. Am I imagining this? Does she know it's me? Maybe this is all just wishful thinking.

"Ashley," Dean Webber calls as he strides over to us. "I want you to meet some more of our newest family members."

She nods and starts to follow him, but not before casting another glance my way. When she looks at me, the uncertainty, the pain I've held on to for so long, temporarily fades away. I want to reach out for her, to take her hand again and this time never, ever let it go.

"What's with you?" Jack counters as I lean away from him, drawing toward her.

I'm Caroline. Tonight, I'm Caroline. I have to play along, so I let myself get pulled away by Jack.

CHAPTER SEVEN

LAST SUMMER

The subway smells like sweat and pee and god knows what else. It's standing room only, and I'm jammed in the middle of a group of guys in American-flag muscle tees wearing their sunglasses on the backs of their necks, pregaming for the Fourth of July fireworks. My earplugs are not doing much to drown out their hollering, but still, I can't wipe the smile off my face. Because I'm spending the whole weekend with her.

I walk through the sliding glass doors of her building and approach the front desk. My building doesn't have a doorman, so I'm never quite sure what to say to one.

"Hello!" I greet him cheerfully. "I'm here to see Ash. Uh, Ashley. Webber."

"Sure," he says as he picks up the phone. "I'll let her know you're here. Name please?"

"Waverly."

I rock back and forth on my heels as he calls her. Then he nods and waves me toward the elevators. I use the ride up to wipe my sweaty palms on my pants and adjust my hair in the mirrored wall. The doors open and there she is, beaming at me, and I want to pinch myself.

"Hi," I say, shyly. Ash takes me by the hand and pulls me into her penthouse apartment. Her dad is away for the weekend—some politics thing in Texas to raise money—so we have the whole place to ourselves. She pulls my backpack off my shoulders and lets it fall to the marble floor, and then her lips are on mine and I feel like if she weren't holding me I'd float away. Before I know it, my clothes are joining my backpack on the floor, along with her clothes, and then we're on the couch. My body shakes from nerves, from the newness and the insecurities racing through my mind, but the more she touches me, the safer I feel. And when I touch her, she becomes everything. All I can see and hear and feel and taste is her. The whole world falls away.

When we finally come up for air, fireworks are lighting up the sky over Central Park, illuminating the whole apartment with rainbow sparks.

"Come on," Ash says, tugging her clothes back on. "Let's watch from the rooftop."

"Be right out," I reply. The noise is already fraying my nerves. I hurriedly get dressed, throw on my big headphones, and step outside into the humid summer air. All of Manhattan explodes around us. People are partying on neighboring roofs and balconies, but here, it's just the two of us, in her garden filled with palms and vines and couches, and the world at our feet.

I avoid eye contact with Ash, not wanting to see the judgment in her face when she notices my headphones, even though she's seen me wear them dozens of times before. After all the time we've spent together, getting to know every tiny detail about each other, I still expect her to turn on me, but she never does. When I clap excitedly and flap my hands in response to all the colors in the sky, she doesn't give me a weird look or try to stop me. She smiles. A big, wide smile, the fireworks reflecting in the blue swimming pools of her eyes. She's summer personified. I lean in and kiss her, my hand holding the back of her neck, holding her close. I don't know how I keep wanting more of her, but she's like a sugar rush that won't end. And I hope it never does.

When I wake up the next morning, in Ash's gigantic, fluffy bed, I feel like a new person. The sun shines through her tall windows. I've never woken up to an unobstructed view of the sky before—at home it's just more apartment windows. But there's a sinking feeling in my stomach. This weekend has already been the best I've ever had, but it's not real. Not for me. My world is nothing like this. What happens when Ash sees that?

I take in a deep breath, and the smell of pancakes and bacon drags me out of bed. As I'm pulling on yesterday's clothes, I notice the early-acceptance letter from Harvard sitting proudly on Ash's desk. Acceptance letters from other prestigious schools flooded in, too, but Harvard was her goal—because that's what her dad wants. Anything short of an Ivy League school isn't good enough for Dean Webber's daughter.

That's what matters, I remind myself as I fix my hair in her standing mirror, not the worlds we grew up in: the world we want to create together.

I stumble into the kitchen, my brain a little foggy from the rosé we drank last night, but when I see her everything gets clear. She's wearing a blue RBG T-shirt, tied in the middle to show off her midriff, and baggy flannel pajama pants that look so cozy I want to wrap myself up in her. Her hair is falling out of the messy bun she slept beside me in.

Oh, god. I'm totally in love with this girl.

The realization hits me so hard I lose my breath. I guess it was bound to happen. We've been dating in secret for months—using our "study sessions" to . . . ahem. Not study. FaceTiming each other all hours of the night. Expertly timing our bathroom breaks during class. I let myself get swept up in her orbit. I could spot her freckles in a lineup and recognize the smell of her Chanel perfume from three classrooms away. Falling in love with Ashley Webber was inevitable for me. I'm floating so close to the sun. I just hope I don't get burned.

Just then, Ash turns around and sees me standing there, watching her like a creep, and she smiles.

"You're up!"

She flips—legit flips—a pancake in the air and it lands on a plate. She's magic. "Huh?" she says, looking at me expectantly.

Crap. Did I say that out loud? "Uh. That looks delicious!"

Another beaming smile. "Good, because it's for you." She slides the plate toward me, along with a bottle of pure maple syrup—the expensive kind, not the cheap maple-flavored syrup my parents buy—and my stomach rumbles. But I keep my hands by my sides, resisting the temptation to dig in until Ash is ready to eat, too. It's a rule my mom and dad have drilled into me: Don't start eating a meal until everyone else at the table has their food. As Mom always says, "Manners are free."

Ash stares at me. "Eat! *Mangia, mangia!*" She throws her arms in the air.

"Huh?"

"My nonna used to say it," she explains. "My mom's mom. She died when I was little, a few years before my mom. That's the only Italian I remember. It means eat. Eat up!"

"Oh." I had no idea Ash was Italian. It's rare for her to bring up her mom, so I take it as a sign that she feels comfortable enough with me to share the parts of herself she keeps hidden from everyone else. She's letting me see her, just like I let her see me. If this isn't love, I don't know what is.

So, maybe she's in love with me, too. I take a bite of my bacon and try to calculate how many days, weeks, months is appropriate in a relationship before you can tell someone you love them. Is now too soon? What if she freaks out? What if she doesn't say it back? I would die. What if she does say it back? Again, I would die.

So maybe I should just keep my mouth shut.

"Hey." Ash turns to me with her eyes as big as saucers. "Wanna do something a little adventurous with me today?"

What could be more adventurous than what we were doing last night? "Definitely."

And that's how I end up on a rickety rowboat in the middle
of Central Park Lake later that day. I gotta admit, it's romantic
as hell. Ash packed a cute wicker basket with a baguette, butter, three different kinds of cheese from Eataly, some kind of
fancy crackers, and a six-pack of LaCroix. She's sitting across
from me in the boat in a baby-blue Refinery dress, her blond
hair fluffed around her ears. I feel like I'm the love interest
in a Taylor Swift music video. It'd be all sepia toned and sun
drenched, only I'd be wearing a nice white shirt with sus-
penders and rowing the boat effortlessly instead of protecting
my pale skin under an old flannel as sweat drips down my
butt crack. Other boat couples float by, and I feel like they're
looking at us and wondering what she's doing with me.

I shake my head to get that thought out, but the spinning
doesn't stop. The July sun beats down, and it's like somebody
turned the brightness up to one million. The glare of its reflection on the water gets too loud, like a shrieking only I can
hear. And then the rest of the park turns up the volume, too.
Things I could hear before, but was able to hold back, come
rushing through the breached gates: children on the shoreline
squealing as they catch sight of turtles popping their heads
above water; musicians playing music somewhere behind the
trees; a clown making balloon ani— *POP.*

I drop the oars, and my hands fly up to cover my ears. My
eyes slam shut. I got so caught up in making this weekend

perfect, in having fun and spending every second with Ash, that I wasn't paying attention to my own body overloading. And now it's too late.

"Waverly?" Ash asks. The boat rocks slightly as she moves closer; a panicked hum vibrates in my throat.

"It's too hot" is all I can say. *It's too everything* is what I mean. I want to go. I need to go. But we're on a tiny boat and the only way out is to either swim or row—and both options sound exhausting and impossible. I didn't bring my headphones because I was afraid of what Ash would think, but now I wish I'd brought my headphones, my stim toys, an ice pack, all of it.

"Okay," Ash says. "Um. Do you want to go?"

Yes. I nod. I nod a lot. But my eyes stay shut and my ears stay covered. Without another word, Ash is taking my place, picking up the oars, and rowing us back to the docks. I sink to the floor of the boat and try to let the sound of the water calm me down.

I don't switch off of autopilot mode until we're safely back at Ash's place, and I'm under a blanket on her couch.

"I'm sorry I don't have any weighted blankets," she says. She stands a few feet away, hands clasped, eyes tender. "I'll order some to take to Harvard, so when you visit in the fall, you can be totally comfortable."

Her cheeks flush. So do mine. When I visit in the fall, she said. My heart swells. Not only does she still want me around, she wants to actively take steps to make me more comfortable when I'm around her. When I visit in the fall, we won't have to sneak around in empty classrooms or wait for her dad to go out of town.

"Then," she says, "in the fall. We'll be free. We can be whoever we want to be. No one will be able to control us there."

I smile up at her. I love that we're on the same page, thinking the same things, dreaming the same dreams.

"I love you."

Ohhhh. Shit.

A smile breaks out on her face. "What did you say?"

"Nothing," I mutter, then pretend to immediately fall asleep.

Ash laughs. Suddenly she's next to me on the couch. "I love you, too."

I sleep the whole way through the night and still wake up exhausted, but my insides are a cheesy, swoony mess. She loves me.

I pack my bag and get dressed. Her dad's flight arrives at 9:00 A.M. I have to leave before he gets back. She kisses me goodbye as I step backward onto the elevator, and her smile is all I see as the doors close.

She loves me.

I ride the subway home, the lingering brain fog from my sensory-overload moment yesterday making it hard to stay awake. But it's all good, because she loves me.

I get home and find my parents hunched over the kitchen table, holding paper bills in their hands. They tell me Mom's

MS meds are going way up in price. I tell them we'll figure it out. Everything's okay.

She loves me.

The next morning, I reach for my phone and check my texts. I haven't heard anything from Ash since I left her place. Did I fuck up? Did my panic thing on the boat scare her away?

Seeking a distraction, I open Instagram for my morning dose of dopamine with a twist of comparisonitis. But the first post that pops up is from Ash. And there she is . . . in London.

Photos of her sitting in a first-class seat on the red-eye. Then London Bridge. A swanky hotel room. A caption that just reads: last minute trip to london town. don't wait up!

It has to be an old post. An Insta glitch. A joke I'm not understanding. It can't be real. She loves me.

But then a question enters my mind that I can't shake: What if this is real, and what I thought I had with Ash was the glitch?

If she loves me—

Then why do I never hear from her again?

CHAPTER EIGHT

Y ou want some?" Jack asks as he lifts a gold flask out of his jacket pocket.

I shake my head. The only reason I've stayed on the dance floor with him so long is because I'm supposed to be playing the role of his adoring girlfriend. I can't give anyone a reason to suspect otherwise. Now that people have noticed that "Caroline" has come to the ball after all, they are watching us with intrigue and, probably, morbid curiosity. I hate that my presence has immediately cast Jack as the caring, supportive boyfriend when I know he is, in reality, the exact opposite of that for Caroline. Now that he's let go of me to refuel, I'm taking my chance to escape as casually as possible.

"I need a bathroom break," I say.

He groans. "Fine. But be quick."

I'm on my way off the dance floor when I spot Pari sitting

on one of the couches, taking a break from dancing. Frank is next to her, completely engrossed in a game of chess he's playing with one of his debate club friends. Pari looks bored out of her mind. I smile. Finally, my real friends.

"Cinderella!" Pari exclaims when she sees me. "Have you got your fairy-tale ending yet?"

"This is more like a nightmare," I say, maybe a little dramatically. I glance over my shoulder and see Jack watching me between swigs from his flask.

Pari follows my gaze, then stands up and takes my hand without saying a word. She leads me into the parlor, a blush-pink room with velvet love seats, fur rugs, soft lighting, and dressing tables complete with arched mirrors and complimentary beauty products in Chanel bags. Girls are seated at the mirrors, touching up their makeup, while others lounge and chat and take group photos with Polaroid cameras provided on a marble table. I would live in this room if I could, it's that pretty and Instagrammable. I make a mental note to grab one of the goodie bags before the night is over.

"Have you talked to Ash yet?" is the first thing Pari asks once we find a private booth in a corner.

I shake my head. "Every time I get close, I choke. But I swear she recognized me under this getup. The way she looked at me . . ." I trail off, lost in the memory of her gaze.

"Okay," Pari says. She chews on her bottom lip, and I know she's trying very hard not to say something.

"What?"

She taps her fingers on her cane. "I'm sorry! I just don't trust her. Something is up with that girl."

"I know. I get it." But it hurts. I want Pari to support me, even if I'm making the worst decision of my life. "Help me with this tonight, and then it's over. I just need to know what happened."

Pari's nostrils flare. "Of course I'll help you. I'll hold her down while you interrogate her if I have to. But you gotta actually, like, talk to her first."

I cringe. "It's hard with the jackass stalking me all night. I think he suspects something, and is pushing to see how far he can go before I give up the game."

"That sounds pretty on-brand for Jack."

I slump back into the velvet seating, sinking beneath the fluffy cushions. "I don't know how much longer I can keep this up," I say. "Being Caroline is exhausting. I feel like I'm being watched everywhere I go. People keep whispering and grabbing me. It's creepy as hell. And then! There's this random girl in a green dress who I saw with Ash, and like, who the hell is she? Is she dating someone else?"

"I haven't heard anything about her dating anyone." Pari whips out her phone and opens Instagram, tapping onto Ash's profile. I sit up so fast I knock half the cushions onto the floor and have to pick them up.

It's mostly photos of Ash with textbooks, on the Oxford campus, drinking coffee. Sprinkled throughout are posts from her travels to Paris, Rome, Amsterdam. She's smiling in the selfies, but it never quite reaches her eyes. Or maybe I'm projecting. I've wasted a lot of study time looking at these photos, trying to find clues for why she left without a word, torturing myself daily to check if she's posted anything new that could help me understand.

"No girls in green," Pari says. "No one but Ash."

I shrug. "They were arguing. I couldn't hear what they were saying, but it looked intense."

"That is weird," she says.

"Right?" I almost slide my mask up to run a hand down my face, but I stop myself. I don't want to be recognized. "And Max was trying to tell me—I mean Caroline—some big important secret about Jack, but I lost track of her."

"Wow," Pari says, chuckling. "You've been busy!"

I laugh dryly. "This is turning out to be a lot more complicated than I imagined."

Just then, the girl in green flows past us, her dress trailing behind her. I squeeze Pari's hand, and her eyes narrow as she pieces it together. The girl leaves the parlor through a pink curtain at the back, and Pari jumps to her feet.

"Come on," she says, tugging me along. "Let's find out who this bitch is."

I get up from the couch, and we walk hand in hand through the curtain and into a dark hallway. The girl walks through a set of double doors labeled PRIVATE.

I hesitate. "It says private."

Pari rolls her eyes at me. "So what?"

"So we aren't allowed in there!" I'm a rule follower. Usually. Today isn't a good example of that.

"Come on! We have a mystery to solve!" Pari pulls me through the doors. Her energy is electric. She loves this kind of shit. Getting into trouble is like a drug for her.

I, on the other hand, am shaking like a leaf, a thousand different worries racing through my mind. "This isn't *Scooby-Doo*, Pari."

"Everything is *Scooby-Doo,*" she whispers as we tiptoe down another hallway. "Every episode ends with a rich white dude being unmasked as the villain. How is that not real life?"

She has a point.

"Where'd she go?" Pari asks.

"Maybe she's a ghost," I joke, trying to lighten the mood. The hallway is all scuffed red brick and exposed piping. Industrial light bulbs sit perched on the walls between framed vintage photographs of young women sitting at cramped sewing tables, with pompadoured hair and high-collared dresses. I can't help but stare at the nameless, unsmiling faces as we wander down the hall, wondering what happened to all of them.

"Oh, look," Pari says, her tone thick with snark as she points to one of the photographs. "Exploited immigrant women, used by the grand old Webber daddies to hoard money and influence." She sticks her finger in her mouth in a show of mock gagging.

Pari has always been suspicious of Owen Webber. The day Pari and I met, in ninth grade, we had been called to the library at school for a photo shoot. The dean wanted us on the academy's new website and posters in time for the enrollment period. In exchange, we'd get extra credit to add to our future college applications. Pari was super quiet at first, but so was I. Neither of us were comfortable in the spotlight, and having a photographer ordering us to pose and smile and pretend to read eleventh-grade science books was super weird.

When the photos went up on the website and even on the academy's social media, my parents were so proud. My mom baked the dean a special yellow cake as a thank-you. Pari's parents were just as excited, but Pari was pissed. She cornered me in the commons, waving one of the posters she'd torn off a wall in the administration office.

"You do realize we've been used as props?" she asked me.

I didn't know what she meant. Part of me felt embarrassed when I saw my dorky smile everywhere, but another part of me enjoyed the attention. It felt nice to be chosen by the dean himself to represent such a prestigious school.

"They're using us for public-facing diversity points," Pari had said. "The low-income, queer, autistic scholarship girl and the visibly disabled, bisexual, South Asian girl getting their STEM on together. Now all the liberal white parents can sit in their Brooklyn Heights brownstones and pat themselves on the back for being part of an inclusive school, and they'll add a few extra zeros to their donations to Webber. Meanwhile, where does it say that I'm the only Indian girl in our class? Where does it say your parents have to scrub floors and feed trust-fund kids just so you can go here?"

It was my first time hearing anyone say a negative word about Webber, and it sparked something in me. But I quickly tamped it back down. Even if what Pari said was true, what could we do about it? The photos were already out there, and turning on the dean meant risking my scholarship, my parents' jobs, my whole future. And deep down, I didn't want to believe that someone I had put so much trust in could use me like that, or that I would be foolish enough to fall for it.

So I focused on studying, started tutoring after school, and put all my effort into doing whatever I could to graduate with good grades and everything I needed to get into premed. I couldn't let myself think too hard about what Pari had said. At the end of the day, she's a legacy at Yale. She has her college plans set in stone. Mine depend on the hard work of myself and my parents, and that includes respecting the dean. It may not be a perfect system, but it's the only one we have, and I have to play it right.

The sound of metal scraping against metal screeches through the air, snapping me out of my thoughts. We round a corner just as the vertical doors of a freight elevator close, with the girl in green standing alone inside it.

"There she is," Pari says. She points at the girl. "Hey! Wait up!"

The girl in green ignores her, and the doors close.

I run my fingers over the smooth material of my dress, trying to calm my anxiety. "We should go back to the party."

"Okay," she says. "You go back. I'm following the White Rabbit down the rabbit hole."

She keeps going, and I linger behind, rocking back and forth on my heels. Breaking rules makes me uncomfortable, and my chances of talking to Ash are back in the ballroom. But what kind of person lets their best friend go all *Alice in Wonderland* on their own?

Pari is waiting impatiently by the elevator door when I stand next to her. She looks at me sideways and smirks. "I knew you wouldn't leave me hanging."

There's a ding as the elevator returns, and we know from the lit-up numbers above it that the mystery girl went to the basement, so I press the B button. The doors rumble closed, and the lower we sink, the higher my heart rate rises.

When the doors open again, we're greeted by a mirror that climbs up to the concrete ceiling, with a set of sliding doors in the center. Printed text on the glass reads: WELCOME TO THE FUTURE.

"Vague much?" Pari scoffs.

I really don't want to know what's beyond those doors, but there's nowhere else to go except back where we came, and I know Pari will never give up now.

We step through the doors as they swoop open and blink at the sudden burst of neon lights.

"It's like a rave," Pari says at the same moment I say, "It's like lightsabers."

As my eyes adjust, I realize we're at the entrance to some kind of light show or hall of mirrors. Lasers bounce off the mirrored ceilings and walls, zapping all our reflections and dancing over our skin. This must be what it's like on hallucinogens.

Narrow corners and pathways twist around each other like a glass maze.

"We're never gonna find her in here," I say. Even more reason to retreat.

Pari nudges me with her shoulder and gives me a wicked smile. "Where's your sense of adventure?"

"I don't know," I say, pretending to look around. "Let me go find it." I start heading back for the door, but Pari snatches my arm and pulls me back, laughing.

"Nice try, kid. C'mon!"

And with that, she's off, moving as fast as she can, her cane tap-tapping against the concrete floor.

"Pari!" I call after her, but it's no use over the loud electronic dance music blaring. Crap. This is a recipe for sensory overload. I pull my earplugs out of my dress pocket and slip them in my ears. It muffles the music, but I can still feel the beat booming in my chest. I don't have sunglasses to lessen the intensity of the strobe lights, so I'm just gonna have to grit my teeth and bear it. And breathe. Must remember to breathe.

By the time I feel ready to combat the chaos, Pari is gone. I lift my dress up an inch so I can move faster, then launch myself forward.

The first thing I see once I'm deeper into the maze is a dreamscape projected on a wall. It's a bird's-eye view of Manhattan, the Empire State Building front and center. This must be the "interactive experience" Webber had promised to show the parents in his speech. I keep going and see another projection, this time of the California wildfires, an orange sky burning.

Hurricanes flooding downtown Manhattan and wiping out neighborhoods closest to the water. A high-speed clip of a rose blooming and then shriveling into nothing. Round and round I go like this, the footage growing more and more ominous.

The neon-blue sky over Queens when the transformer exploded at the power plant a few years ago. Buildings destroyed and abandoned. Police attacking protestors. Politicians screaming at each other from podiums. Hospital workers in hazmat suits as they care for patients on ventilators. A pile of old television sets in an empty warehouse, the screens showing different cable news stations before going to static and ending with the words SYSTEM FAILURE flashing on them. Then a mushroom cloud. Reels and reels of chaos and pain on loop all around me.

The words on the entrance to this ninth circle of hell said this was the future, but it's not. It's the past and the present, the world as I've always known it to be. Why would the dean want to bombard his donors and friends and academy family with the horrors of our world like this? It's almost like he's trying to frighten them. And if they're anything like me, it's working. My heart feels like it's trying to climb out of my throat.

I keep going, when suddenly I'm at the center of the maze.

CHAPTER NINE

Dozens of rows of theater-style chairs sit facing a bare white wall. I stop, trying to catch my bearings and my sanity. I only intend to stay for a second, but the wall flickers to life, and the words THE NEW WORLD appear on it. A short film starts to roll, showing a forest. Lush green trees. Birds bathing in a stream.

Then white people—hetero families with moms and dads and children—sitting in a circle together in a field of wildflowers. The women dressed in feminine floral dresses with wide sun hats. The men in cashmere sweaters over collared shirts and beige khakis. They're all smiles and laughter and rosy cheeks. It's like an Anthropologie ad. Or *Midsommar*.

Then, children draw with crayons at kitchen tables while mothers wash dishes in the sink and smile lovingly. Cheerful teachers calling on enthusiastic students in a classroom. Men in crisp white lab coats peering into microscopes and grinning proudly.

It's like watching a Best of Stock Footage video, but for some reason it's being framed as a promise for a new world. The kind of world Webber likes to talk about. And it gives me the creeps. There are no people of color, there are no queer folks, no disabled people. Everyone is thin, white, cisgender, straight, and smiling.

There's no home for me there. No home for my friends, my parents, not even Webber's own daughter. What happens to people like us if we end up in a place like that?

I've had enough of this. I try to shake off everything I've seen as I turn left, then right, then left again. It's like I'm trapped inside a mirror ball, lights ricocheting off of glass, flying across the ceiling like shooting stars. I clutch my mask to my face and close my eyes, trying to settle my disoriented mind. This night has been entirely Too Much.

Suddenly, the maze falls silent. All I can hear is the ringing in my own ears. I open my eyes, and everything is pitch-dark. Not a single stream of light.

"Waverly?" I hear Pari call. Her voice is muffled through my earplugs, but she sounds close.

"Pari!" I call back. I take out my earplugs and listen. "Where are you?"

"No idea, bro!" she says with a nervous laugh. "Not a fan of this hellscape, though!"

I reach a hand out and find the cool, flat surface of the glass, then shuffle alongside it in the direction of Pari's voice.

"I'm coming!" I yell out to her, but she doesn't answer. Footsteps come up behind me, and I freeze. "Pari?"

Silence.

My skin prickles with sweat and goose bumps. I hate this. I hate this so freaking much.

The lights flash on for a split second, and I swear I see someone standing behind me in the mirror before darkness falls over me again.

"Oh, fuck this." I'm not standing around in the dark waiting to be murdered. I spin around so my back is against the glass, then slide against it as I continue through the maze, using it to help navigate my way.

Again, the footsteps follow. Slower. Lighter. Like whoever it is is trying to be quiet. High heels click on the concrete floor, getting closer and closer even though I'm moving faster and faster.

The lights spark to life, lasers cutting through the darkness haphazardly, music blasting so loud I drop my earplugs and have to cover my ears. And then I see her, the girl in green. She's standing directly in front of me, staring.

The lights flicker again, and she disappears, like a ghost or a figment of my imagination. Maybe this really is a nightmare. Maybe I'm sound asleep in my bed at home, having an intense anxiety dream about the masquerade. Maybe none of this is actually real. Or, maybe, I've officially lost my mind.

Either way, I'm very much done with this psychedelic trip. I get down on the floor and feel around for my earplugs, sweat beading under my mask and down my neck. Everything is so loud it hurts.

"Yes!" I find them, quickly dust them off and slip them back in my ears, and start running to get the hell out. I hit a dead end and get startled by my own reflection, but when I turn back I reach a different section. It's one long glass wall, and through it I can see Pari waiting outside the maze, sitting in a shadowy corner, her dress puffed around her like a cloud, cane resting on her lap. Her head bops up and down slightly; she's probably listening to music on her contraband phone. How the hell did she get there? And how is she so damn chill?

I try to get her attention by waving, calling her name, jumping up and down. But even though she seems to be looking right at me, it's like I'm invisible. And that's when I realize: this wall is a one-way mirror. I can see her, but she can't see me. I slam my hands against the glass and yell. It does nothing; it's like I don't even exist.

Every way I look, the path just leads me back deeper into the maze. This glass wall is all that separates me from freedom. How can I be so close yet so far away?

Just then, the girl in green appears from the far right of the room, on the other side of the glass. She made it out! What the hell? My breath grows shallow, and it feels like the walls are closing in on me.

I squint through the flashing lights, my gaze following her as she steps up to a red curtain marking the exit—not the way we came in, but a deeper section of the factory. She pulls the curtain to the side and startles. The giant security guard with the gold angel mask—the guy who took our phones at the door—appears, all broad shoulders and a tux so tight his arm muscles risk bursting right through the material. He nods at her and motions for her to step inside.

Pari has noticed. She leverages her weight on her cane to stand up, then struts toward the guard like a VIP.

I slam my hands on the wall again as she goes by, screaming her name as loud as I can. She doesn't even flinch in my direction. It's like I'm a ghost trying to get the attention of the living.

Straight-shouldered and confident, Pari tries to walk straight past the guard, but he steps in front of her, shaking his head. Pari's hand moves to her hip. I can't hear what she's saying, but I bet it's badass.

The guard shakes his head again, this time crossing his arms over his buff chest as an extra show of force. Pari takes a step closer, craning her neck to look up at him.

They stay like that for a good thirty seconds, neither of them giving an inch. Then, seemingly admitting defeat, Pari shrugs, turns around, and starts walking away. I let out a sigh of relief. The guard starts talking into his headset and lets the curtain close in front of him.

I thought for sure Pari had given up, but the next thing I know, she's turning around and running back to the curtain. Instinctively, I hold my breath, because I know it must cause her pain to move that fast. She almost makes it through, but the guard is too quick. He catches her by the arm and doesn't let go. My heart hammers as Pari struggles against him, hitting his chest with a clenched fist. He winces, but keeps his grip on her other wrist.

I slam my hands onto the glass wall, screaming at him to let her go. They don't notice.

He waggles his index finger in Pari's face and says something to her, then motions behind him with his thumb. She shrugs nonchalantly, almost like she's daring him to do whatever he just threatened her with. It works. He tightens his hold on her and takes her behind the curtain. I burst into a sprint, following the godforsaken maze, praying for an exit. I run and run until I'm almost out of breath.

Then I see it: another set of sliding doors. The words THE END sparkle across it.

Finally.

I race through and make a beeline for the curtain. The moment I'm through them, I hear Pari's sarcastic voice, and pull my earplugs out.

"So the random white girl in the green dress gets VIP treatment," she's saying. "But the brown girl gets taken into custody? How original!"

"You need a time-out, young lady," a brutish voice replies.

I start to move toward their voices, but the dimly lit private corridors of the factory are as confusing and mazelike as the light show.

"'Young lady'? 'Time-out'? What is this, kindergarten?" Pari yells from somewhere farther away. "Unhand me!"

I pick up my pace, trying to catch up, but I reach a fork in the hallways and don't know which way to go.

"Pari!" I call out, but all I hear in return is the sound of my own voice echoing back at me.

I've lost her.

And now I'm lost, too.

"Shit. Shitshitshit." I start pacing up and down the hallway. Flick my wrists, flap my hands, shake my shoulders out. Moving helps me think.

Going back is not an option—that maze almost sent me into a panic attack, and it's the only thing on the other side of those curtains. But I can't just wait around here either; that guard could be back any second. I need to keep going. *Just pick a direction, Waverly. Make a goddamn decision.*

But what if I choose wrong?

The chandeliers hanging from the ceiling switch off. My breath catches in my throat.

Just then, a hand clutches my arm and spins me around. I scream loud enough to make whoever it is jump back and let go of me. The lights come back to life. It's the girl in green. She grabs my hands. I try to place her eyes behind the mask, but it's still too dark and disorienting to focus.

"Get out of here," she whispers.

I don't move. She digs her long fingernails into my palms. "Go! Run for your life!"

She pushes me away, and I run. When I glance back over my shoulder, she's gone. The hall fades from darkness to light and back again, and I look up at the row of chandeliers just as they get so bright it hurts my eyes.

BOOM.

The chandelier explodes, sending glass showering behind me like a hailstorm. I barely outrun the tiny knives slicing through the air, screaming every time there's another burst of electricity as they explode one by one above me. The freight elevator sits open at the end of the hall, and I skid to a stop inside it, grateful for shelter. The doors close and the elevator jerks to life, moving down below the basement level to somewhere even deeper and darker.

Before I can panic about going in the wrong direction, the elevator shakes to a stop. The lights go out. Everything gets quiet. I'm stuck.

"Are you serious?" I shout to no one. Can this night get any worse? I cup my hands over my mouth and start yelling for help.

"Hello?" I call. "Is anyone there? I need some help, please! Hello?"

Nothing.

I peek through a gap between the doors. My view is partially blocked by the grimy steel tracks that guide the elevator, but just below that is the opening to a lower-level landing. Beyond that, all I see is darkness. I either stay here and wait for this metal box to take me down to hell, or I slide out.

I hate to admit it, but I consider staying in here for the rest of the night. Clearly, this building hates me. It's a living entity, and it knows I'm not supposed to be roaming inside its walls. This is my punishment for lying; I'm stuck here until some guard finds me, and Pari will think I abandoned her. The dean will learn of my lies and sneaking around and expel me from school. My college dreams will be dashed. My chances of talking to Ash will be destroyed.

A disturbing creaking sound rings out from somewhere above me, and in my mind I imagine the old wires suspending me in midair snapping clean. If I'm going to make a move, it has to be now.

I pry the doors apart, gritting my teeth and working up a sweat that will definitely stain this dress. The awful screech it makes travels up the elevator shaft and pierces my bones. I wonder if anyone is around to hear it.

Once it's wide enough to fit through, I gather my skirt up around my knees so it doesn't catch on anything and slide my legs through the opening. The elevator hangs so precariously positioned that I have to lie flat on my stomach to push myself out backward, then basically fall the rest of the way. The drop must be at least five feet, and it's too dark to see what, exactly, I'll be landing on. An intrusive image flashes in my mind of the elevator springing to life and slicing me in half, but I keep going.

I kick my heels off, and they fall to the floor, the sound echoing. My biceps flex and strain as I lower myself down farther and farther, until my toes touch the cool surface below. It feels like concrete. I suck in a deep breath, then let go.

In true Waverly fashion, I do not stick the landing.

I trip on my own shoes and stumble backward onto my butt, then my elbows, then my head. Once I'm on the floor, I embrace it for a moment, taking some time to catch my breath. At least I'm still in one piece. Drops of sweat run down my face, and I tear my mask off. I'm really starting to hate this disguise, but now that I'm free of that death box, I have more important things to worry about, like finding Pari and getting back to the party and talking to Ash.

Something hard digs into my back, and I reach under myself to find a dusty old flashlight. Finally, something goes my way! I flip the switch and sigh in relief when it lights up. I stand up, turn around, and point the flashlight in front of me. Then I scream.

A lifeless face stares back at me, unmoving. A mannequin. I pan the light across the vast, shadowy room and see hundreds of mannequins in different states of decay. This must be some kind of storeroom for the old sewing figures they used back in the day.

My whole body shakes. This is without a doubt the scariest sight I've ever seen. And now I'm trapped down here with these creepy things.

Fuck—and I cannot stress this enough—my life.

CHAPTER TEN

'm standing alone in a deep dark factory storeroom with hundreds of rotting mannequins and headless torsos. I don't know what horror movie I've just stepped into, but I'm not sticking around to see how it ends. Slowly, I back up toward the elevator, deciding I'd rather take my chances in a hanging metal box than try to navigate this mess.

But just as I'm about to climb back inside, it roars to life, the sudden noise making me jump. I watch, wide-eyed and terrified, as the doors close and the elevator disappears back up, up, up, leaving me here alone.

"Okay," I whisper to myself. "Don't panic. This is fine. I can handle this." I search the wall for the button to bring the elevator back down, but when I press it, it falls off and hits the floor with a metal clang. The sound echoes around me, and then I hear a chilling scurrying noise that makes me want to crawl into a ball and die.

I turn to face the murder statues again. They stare at me, smiling, mocking me. The flashlight shining on them casts tall shadow figures on the walls. The hairs on the back of my neck rise up; my skin prickles into a cold sweat. What do I do now? There's no way I'm waiting down here in this secret underground society of crumbling mannequins for someone to find me. And if I ever make it out of here, no one's ever going to believe this story.

Wait. Did that mannequin just move its head? I swear it was facing the other way a second ago. Shit. My mind has already started playing tricks on me. Something rustles in the distance. I hold my breath, trying to listen for where the noise is coming from. But all I can hear is my own thumping heartbeat. Maybe I imagined it.

I huff out a breath and shake off my paranoia.

There has to be another way out of here. I scan the room and catch a thin ray of light streaming through a crack on the far side. *Please, please, please be a door.*

"This is fine," I say again. Then I push myself forward, weaving through the plastic bodies. "Totally, completely, one hundred percent fine."

I secure the mask back to my face like it's a shield. Then, keeping the flashlight trained on the floor just in front of me, I focus on taking one step at a time, and definitely don't think about the painted eyeballs following me as I move. The skirt of my dress is so wide that it pushes into some of them, making them wobble, the movement making me yelp when I see it in the corner of my vision.

"Still fine," I say to myself. "So very fine." I start humming to myself, trying to calm myself with a verbal stim.

A scratching sound from behind makes me stop dead in my tracks. What the hell was that? I decide looking back is a very bad idea and start walking again, only to hear the scratching sound to my right this time.

I laugh, because it's the only reaction I can muster to calm myself down. "Okay, no thank you." I pick up my pace, but the scratching sound follows me like a shadow. And then I feel it, tiny little claws running over my shoe. I jump into the air, knocking over a bald-headed mannequin. It tumbles into another one, and then a bunch of them all fall like dominoes. The ruckus scares the little community of rats living down here, and they scatter all around me.

I scream and run and then scream some more, my arms flailing wildly, knocking over every mannequin in my way. I don't stop until I've reached the crack of light that is now my only hope.

"Please," I whimper. A handle reflects against the light of my flashlight. A door!

But when I try to open it, it's stuck. I drop the flashlight so I can take the handle with both hands, and as it clatters to the floor, it shines on a giant rat right next to me. I'm screaming so much now it's practically echoing through the whole building. I give one big tug on the door, and it finally opens, scraping against the concrete floor. A stairwell.

I jump inside and slam the door shut behind me, taking a moment to calm myself down. I close my eyes and shake my whole body like a rag doll, trying to shake off the feeling of phantom rats crawling all over my skin.

The staircase is made of stone and spirals up into the darkness. Weak reddish lighting makes it look like the only stairwell out of hell, and after where I've just been, it feels like it, too. It reminds me of secret passageways from movies about castles and grand old mansions.

Once my heart rate has slowed a little and I've stopped hyperventilating, I start climbing.

After a few flights, I'm breathing hard when I reach a heavy door and push it open. I step into a cloud of smoke and dim orange-hued lighting. The door slams shut behind me, and I realize it wasn't a door at all. From this side, in the room, the door is a bookcase. I've entered through a secret door. The stairwell looked like a secret passageway because it *was* a secret passageway. And now I'm stuck here—wherever here is.

Cigar smoke fills the air. Brown leather couches and armchairs sit on the edges of a classical red rug. Built-in bookshelves made of rich wood house vintage books, antique globes of the Earth, and little brass statues of greyhounds and horses. A fake but grand fireplace sits opposite to where I entered, a copper basket of wood and fire pokers in front of it. Above the mantel hangs a portrait of Owen Webber, Sr., wearing a suit of armor, posing with his foot on the head of a lion. Real suits of armor flank the fireplace, complete with swords. Smaller knives and thin blades hang proudly on the walls, next to dead-eyed busts of woodland creatures. Deer, fox, and some kind of hairy pig. Gross.

I've stepped into an old boys' club, the kind of place where men brag about their sexual and financial conquests over expensive bottles of whiskey. Needless to say, this is not where a gay, disabled teenage girl from a poor family belongs. I am not safe here. In a room like this, add a bunch of boys and suddenly I'm just like the deer on the wall. This is how white girls end up the focus of a true crime podcast. I need to get out of here before I get caught.

I creep toward the main door, but before I even take two steps, the handle turns. Someone's coming.

Panicked, I flip myself behind the nearest couch and drop between it and a wall—one with medieval swords displayed proudly on it. I crawl under the couch, tucking the last of my skirt under myself, feeling terrible for crushing Caroline's beautiful dress.

The ribs of the couch's underside dig into my shoulder blades, but there's nothing I can do. Getting busted in a private men's club area will surely get me kicked out of the party—not to mention a stern phone call to my parents. Oh, god, what if Webber kicks me out of school? No other private school would accept me. I'd be blacklisted. Coming to this party has put my whole future on the line. What the hell was I thinking?

Men's voices fill the room. I swallow my anxiety down as they scatter around me; I can see their shined shoes against the plush carpet, feel their weight pressing against me as they sit down on the couch. It's like they're pressing the air out of me. Others stand nearby, leaning on the bookshelves and talking loudly.

I recognize some of the voices. There's the dean, who is doing most of the talking. Another is Jack's dad, Dr. Bradley. I remember his voice from C-SPAN, when he had to testify before Congress to explain the hike in his company's drug prices. Then there's Congressman George, the reason Bradley didn't face any consequences.

I inch forward ever so slightly, craning my neck to peek out from behind the leg of the couch. From where I am, I can only see three people: Police Commissioner Morrison; the giant security guard who took Pari, standing by the door; and someone else.

Ash.

What is she doing here? She was always so bored by her dad's friends, and now she's here with them as they light cigars and pour themselves whiskey. This is too weird.

"Don't you see?" someone asks. I don't recognize his voice. "His guilt contributed to what happened. And he should feel guilty—we all should!"

The image of Gregory in his office flashes in my mind. One of the men sitting on the couch above me starts tapping his foot, the nervous energy vibrating in my bones. I try to slide back again, worried that someone will see me.

"Jeff," someone says. "Relax. What happened to Gregory doesn't change anything. Caroline is here. She's the key. Everything is still going according to plan."

What. The. Fuck?

Caroline is the key to what? And what happens if they find out Caroline is not, in fact, here? That it's just the queer

scholarship kid from Queens? What the hell has Caroline gotten me into?

The man called Jeff doesn't seem to calm down. I see his
legs pacing back and forth along the rug. "Cassandra told us
this was going to happen. We could have warned people!"

Wait.

Cassandra.

Caroline's dad said the same thing on the phone, and he
was freaking out, too.

Someone steps in front of Jeff, standing very close. "We
can't save everyone." It's Dean Webber. "But we can save ourselves. It's our duty. Don't you see? There's a reason only *we*
have Cassandra, her genius. We are the prepared ones, the ones
who deserve to survive. The sun is going to cleanse the planet.
And when the time is right, we'll reap the benefits. We will
emerge and build a new world!"

Um.

What?

A chill rushes down my spine. My palms feel clammy. I've
never heard Dean Webber talk like this before.

Sure, he loves talking about making the world a better
place, but no more than every wealthy businessman with Silicon Valley connections. But this "cleansing the planet" sounds
kind of woo-woo. Cultish, even. Maybe his obsession with
clean living and vibrations and all that is getting to his head.

It does fit with the doomsday reels playing in that trippy
maze. I don't remember any mention of this Cassandra person
in those clips, though.

I listen as he reassures Jeff, but I swear I can hear Jeff's last thread of hope unraveling. I'm clearly missing huge pieces of the puzzle, because I have no idea what Dean Webber is talking about. Or how Caroline fits into all of this.

Maybe Webber has been working too hard. He doesn't sound like himself.

Jeff steps back. "Do you hear yourself? Do you all hear this?" No one else says a word. "You've all been drinking the Kool-Aid too long. Well, not me! Not anymore. When I agreed to this, I thought we'd be helping people. But you're only in it for yourselves. I've got to get out of here. There's still time to tell people."

Two heavy feet step behind Jeff, blocking him from moving any farther. The next thing I hear is a loud crack, and Ash letting out a muffled scream. Then, *THUD*. Jeff collapses to the floor, his head landing opposite mine on the rug, eyes wide open but completely blank. I bite hard on my bottom lip to stop my own scream from ringing out.

CHAPTER ELEVEN

Owen Webber wasn't supposed to be at my scholarship interview. According to the academy website, the financial aid forms I'd filled out, and all the googling I had done, it would just be me and a member of the admissions team. Her name was Claire. She was white, in her mid-fifties, married to a woman, and ran the library on campus. I still, to this day, think I owe my whole school career to the fact that I spent half of our meeting getting excited with her about books. The way she lit up when I told her about the Little Free Library I helped start in my neighborhood—I knew that had to be a good sign.

But then, completely unannounced, Dean Owen Webber walked in. I'd only ever seen him in photos online, where he was posing with world leaders and at soup kitchens. Being an avid believer in the power of research, I'd read all about him in *The New York Times, Inc., Forbes, TechCrunch;* even *Teen Vogue* and *BuzzFeed* had written pieces praising his work with women-run startups, leadership on liberal issues, raising money for his foundation, and handing out those giant novelty checks.

So when the door opened and he strutted over to me, wearing a classy three-piece suit and a smile, I almost died. Everything went kind of blurry after that, but I remember he knew my name already, and he was impressed with my ambitions to work in medicine. He told me how his wife had died suddenly of a brain aneurysm, and that medical research and science were fields that were close to his heart.

Later, Ash would tell me that the aneurysm struck in her sleep, that her dad woke up to find his wife wasn't breathing, and that he has never slept through the night since. He never forgave himself for being sound asleep next to her while she died, and that was when he turned his focus to trying to control everything, including Ash's life.

I shrugged his control issues off as normal helicopter-parent stuff. Wealthy, WASPy parents are all like that. I couldn't see the true Dean Webber behind the smiling photo ops, the great press headlines, the generosity he showed my family.

But I've finally seen behind the mask, and it's horrifying.

Blood pools around Jeff's skull. A fire poker drops to the floor next to him, pieces of scalp and hair and blood sticking to its sharpest edges. I squeeze my eyes shut and try to count to five as I breathe, trying to stop myself from throwing up. My body starts to shake, and I feel the tips of the crown on my mask poke into the couch, trapping my head.

The two guys sitting on the couch above stand quickly

to avoid the blood, lessening the weight on my back, but it doesn't do anything to ease the pounding panic squeezing my chest. I've never seen someone die before. Let alone be murdered by people I had trusted. People who, now, don't seem to give a shit.

"Mason," Dean Webber says sharply. "You got blood on me."

A deep voice responds. "Sorry, boss. I'll clean it up." The guard. The one who took Pari. He just killed someone right in front of me. In front of everyone in this room. The only people having a normal, human reaction to the literal murder that just occurred are me and Ash, who is sobbing in the corner.

"Jesus, Owen," Congressman George says. "Hasn't your man heard of plausible deniability? We're all witnesses now!"

Webber laughs. "Don't act like you don't lie every day of your life, Congressman."

"That's beside the point," he replies. "I will not be party to murder. I never signed up for that."

"Hey," Dr. Bradley says. "We signed up to do whatever Owen needs."

The congressman yells at Bradley to shut up, and Webber intervenes. "Calm yourselves, gentlemen. This is nothing more than another little blip. It doesn't change a thing."

"A little blip?" the congressman repeats. "That little blip is leaking brains all over your rug, Owen."

Bile rises in my throat, and I force it back down.

"No matter," Webber says. "We're leaving all this behind soon enough. And if you and your family still want to join us, Congressman, you'll need to relax. We're almost across the finish line."

Congressman George doesn't respond, and I assume that means he's decided to back down.

"As for my shirt, Mason, have one of your men switch with me. I have another speech to give soon, and I want to look presentable for the people."

"Whatever you need, boss," Mason says.

"And clean up this mess." I see Webber's shiny shoes step over Jeff's lifeless body, and everyone else in the room follows dutifully. The last words I hear are from the dean as he tells Ash to toughen up.

"These are the kinds of decisions we have to make from now on," he says to his daughter. Her sobs don't ease. "You can't be so emotional. They'll see it as a weakness."

The door creaks closed, but Mason is still in the room with me. His heavy footsteps shake the floor, his grunting loud and aggressive as he lifts Jeff's legs and starts dragging him away like trash.

The red lake of blood seeps through the carpet and runs closer to me, licking at my trembling fingertips. The metallic smell hits, and I gag again. I hold my breath and inch away from it until I can't move any farther. If I don't get out from under this couch soon, I'm worried I'm going to throw up or scream or have a full-blown panic attack. And the way I'm stuck so close to the scene of a murder, I'm going to be stained with the blood of a dissenter, and I'll never make it out of this ball without being exposed.

The sound of the door slamming shut makes me jump, hitting my head against the hard bottom of the couch. But the sudden jolt pulls my mask free from where it was stuck, and I hurriedly slide out from under the couch. I try to stand up, but I'm hit with an intense light-headedness that knocks me back down to the floor. My lips start to tingle, my arms and legs feel numb, and my breathing is so shallow I'm getting dizzy.

Shit. Here comes the panic attack.

My hands push deep into the pockets of my dress, searching for the Just In Case anxiety pill I brought with me. I find the Xanax and pop it in my mouth; the tiny saving grace tastes bitter on my tongue and I force it down my throat.

A doctor prescribed a bottle of them after I had a pretty public meltdown during an exam last year. It was just after Ash had ghosted, and my parents were on the phone all hours of the night arguing with their health insurance about the new medication prices, and I hadn't been able to focus on school or tutoring or anything. It was like I completely shut down. I could hardly speak; it took all my energy just to take a shower. Then I sat down to do an exam I hadn't prepped for, and boom, everything hit me like a tsunami of pain.

So Dad rushed me to urgent care, and a doctor diagnosed me as "anxious," and like, obviously I knew that already. I got the Xanax, but I've only taken two since then (one on another exam day and the other on Christmas Day, when we visit my aunt's house and see all the relatives and it's all just so loud). I hate taking them because it reminds me of that awful day when I lost control—not to mention the guilt it brings up that my parents had to pay for these when they couldn't pay for Mom's last bottle of MS meds.

I sit with my back against the couch, my knees pressed tight against my chest, and start rocking back and forth.

My lungs feel suffocated from fear and cigar smoke and the sickening scent of the blood, so I tear my mask off fully and try to breathe. And then the sobs pour out of me like a storm.

I wish I'd never come to this ridiculous ball. I wish I were at home, sitting in the living room with my parents watching a movie and eating ice cream like we do every Friday night. God, I hope they aren't worried about me. I hope I make it out of here to hug them again.

Everything that has happened in the last couple of hours hits me hard, crushing me like a steamroller. I start questioning everything.

Maybe that wasn't real. Maybe I hit my head when I fell from the elevator and this is all a bad concussion dream. Maybe that laser maze was really a portal into an alternate universe, one where Dean Webber is evil and has people killed.

Or maybe he's just not the man I thought he was.

Could Webber be just as bad as Bradley? Even more so? He wouldn't be the first person to hide crime and corruption behind philanthropy and progressive politics. But that would mean that he doesn't care. About the school. About the people in it. About any of it. He gave me my shot, I thought he actually saw me. Now I wonder if any of it was ever real.

I think of my parents, about how they work themselves to the bone out of pure loyalty and gratitude to Webber. How they put all their trust and energy and money into Webber Academy. The way they talk about him, like he saved our little family from poverty and saved me from a future of struggle and uncertainty.

And I'm the reason they worship him like they do. I'm the one who chose Webber Academy. I researched it, applied for the scholarship, convinced my parents that it was the only way for me to get into Yale with financial aid. I showed them all the great reviews of the school and the impressive profiles of Owen Webber in magazines.

Oh, god. Pari has been right about him the whole time. The pit in my stomach grows. Mason took Pari, and now I know he's capable of murder. I have to find her.

The lights flicker again. This time I can hear it, too. A low buzzing, like the building is whining as it struggles to stay awake. What the hell is going on? Bad wiring? Another blue-sky explosion in Queens?

I'd chalked up the random blackouts over the last few weeks to just Con Ed prepping the grid for a hot summer. They always cut off power to the poorer neighborhoods in Queens and Brooklyn so the Upper East Side folks can run their wine fridges and charge their Teslas. But this factory is in the Seaport area in downtown Manhattan. They'd never do rolling blackouts here; otherwise they'd face the wrath of wine-mom brunch clubs and dudebros from the Financial District.

Whatever is causing the power glitches, maybe it's not Con Ed this time. An uneasy feeling falls over me. The last thing

I want is to be trapped here in the dark, so I urge myself up. Slowly, I crawl onto my knees and peek over the top of the couch, and that's when I see him.

Mason.

I don't know how long he's been standing there, over the stained rug, but he's staring down at me with fierce, wide eyes behind his mask. The angel sitting atop the mask seems to glare at me, too. He's seen my face—my real, tearstained face, unmasked. He moves his hand to his Taser gun and I flinch.

And then darkness hits us again. I take my chances and jump over the couch, running through the shadows and reaching for the door. My hands fumble for the handle as Mason takes loud strides toward me. He must trip, because I hear a thud that shakes the floor beneath me. I find the doorknob and rush out of the room just as the lights spark to life again.

This has to be the husbands-only quarters. The cigar-room aesthetic just won't quit, with the heads of more deer, wolves, even a goddamn moose, watching with dead eyes from the walls. A long, mahogany bar sits to the left, three pool tables in the middle and long leather couches to the right. A giant taxidermy black bear towers over the fathers of Webber Academy as they drink, play, and talk loudly, so engrossed in their own cheering about the lights being back on that they don't notice me running through the room. I hold my mask over my face just in case—I can't risk anyone else seeing who I really am.

I make it out and keep rushing through the corridors, praying that Mason didn't see which way I went. My face drips with sweat and condensation under my mask, and my feet ache as I sprint. High heels were a very bad idea.

Finally, I see a sign that says GRAND BALLROOM and follow the arrow over an enclosed walkway connecting the buildings. When I burst through the double doors into the room, I've never been so happy to see all my classmates.

In the middle of the dance floor, towering over everyone and dancing with his eyes closed, is Frank. I pat my frazzled hair down and tie my mask on properly, trying to at least look like I'm not at my wit's end, and hurry over to him.

"Frank!" I call out to him over the music, and he turns to me with a big smile.

"Where's Pari?" he asks, looking around me. "I haven't seen her in, like, an hour."

"I don't know," I say in between shallow breaths. "But we need to find her. And then we need to get the hell out of here."

Someone taps my shoulder, and I turn around to see Congressman George staring down at me. I freeze up. Oh, god, he must know I was in the cigar room. I'm dead.

"Caroline," he says, his voice low and serious. "You did the right thing by coming here tonight. With what happened to your father, none of this is possible without you now."

Before I can muster up a response, he walks away.

"Uhh," Frank starts. "Is it me, or was that weird?"

"It was weird," I say. "Everything about that guy and this party is weird as fuck. Come with me."

I take his hand and pull him behind the stage, checking to make sure no one sees us. Frank laughs nervously.

"If I didn't know you were a big lesbian," he says, "I'd think you were about to make out with me." His awkward laughter continues.

"I just saw a guy get murdered," I blurt out.

Frank stops laughing. I think he even stops breathing.

"Sorry," I say. The pacing starts again as I launch into a rant, trying to stay quiet. "That was abrupt, but I don't know how to gently bring it up and my brain is still trying to process the whole thing. I probably have PTSD now, right? Oh, god. That's a lot of therapy. I can't afford that. I took a Xanax but I'm not sure if it's working because I still feel like my heart is trying to claw its way out of my chest and my hands are jittery. But maybe it is working, like maybe if I didn't take it I'd be passed out from shock back in the cigar room still, ya know?"

Frank comes back to life and starts pacing alongside me. "Okay, Waverly? Did you take anything else with that Xanax?"

I stop in my tracks, glaring at him. "No, Frank."

He holds his palms up. "Whoa, okay. I had to ask. Now, I need you to back up. Tell me what happened."

I take in a deep breath and try to explain the horrors of the night as calmly and clearly as possible. "There was a girl in a green dress fighting with Ash. Uh. I guess I may as well tell you that Ash and I dated, before she moved to London. Anyway, they were fighting. Pari and I followed the girl in green, trying to find out who she was. We ended up in this mindfuck of a maze that should definitely have a seizure warning, and then Pari was taken away by that buff security guard, Mason. Remember him because he comes back later in a big way."

I pause to take a breath, and to try to read Frank's facial expression behind his mask. His brows are pinched, eyes narrowed, fingers tapping on his chin. He's listening.

"Then there were some explosions and the girl in green came back and disappeared again; I got stuck in an elevator of doom; then I had to run through a mannequin dungeon and escaped into the cigar room—which is where I saw Dean Webber and Mason kill someone."

Hearing myself say it all out loud, it sounds more like the plot of an *American Horror Story* episode than reality. I bite my bottom lip and quietly pray that Frank believes me. I need him on my side.

"Who did they kill?" he asks.

"Jeff," I say, knowing the name sounds familiar but unable to connect the dots with my overwhelmed brain.

Frank's mouth falls open. "Jeff Ramsey? The tech giant?"

Of course! The new guy in Webber's boys' club. Suddenly the face I've seen in photos online matches the face I saw lying on the carpet. My stomach turns. "Yes. That was him. He didn't want to go along with some big plan Webber and the other guys have for 'cleansing the world' tonight."

"Cleansing the world?" Frank repeats, sounding disgusted. "When people like Webber say things like that, it's never good."

I nod. "And they were talking about some woman named Cassandra. I heard Gregory talking about her, too."

"Who is she?"

"No idea. But whoever she is, she has them convinced that some new world is coming, like, now."

Suddenly, it feels like it's a thousand degrees in here, and I can't get Jeff's face out of my mind. He has kids. Little kids who are here tonight. His wife could be right here in the ballroom, wondering where her husband is.

I step closer to the brick wall, push my mask up into my hair, buckle over, and hurl onto the floor. Some of it splatters onto my dress and shoes, but they don't seem to matter so much anymore.

I feel Frank's hand gently patting my back, and I don't have the heart to tell him it just makes me feel worse. I squeeze my eyes shut, let it happen, and hope I'm not puking up my Xanax.

Once I'm done, I straighten up, wipe my face on the back of my hand, and turn back to face Frank. He's trying to act cool, and at some point he got me a bottle of water, which I take and drink gratefully. But his face is paler than I've ever seen it.

"We should go to the police," he says.

I shake my head. "No way. Commissioner Morrison was right there! He did nothing. Didn't even say a word. Webber owns the police, we can't trust them."

Frank's shoulders fall, deflated.

"We can't trust *any* of the adults," I say. "They could all be in the dean's pocket. Besides, no one would believe me if I told them. You heard my story! And Webber, he's their hero." I wince a little. He was my hero only an hour ago, too. If I were them, I probably wouldn't believe me either. Thank god for Frank, who knows I'd never make this up.

He runs a hand over his face. "So what do we do?"

I peek out from behind the stage, onto the dance floor. All the students are dancing, laughing, flirting, having the time of their lives. Meanwhile, somewhere in this building is a dead body, and the man in control of everything is up to something worth killing for. And Pari. Pari is trapped somewhere in these walls, alone.

"We need to find Pari," I say. "I don't know what we'll do after that, but whatever happens, we can't leave her behind. She's my best friend."

He nods. "Agreed. We have to find her."

We head back into the crowd, and I feel a new sense of determination.

And then, as if the factory senses our rebellion, the power goes out.

It's not just a flicker this time. The music screeches to a halt. Gasps ring out from the crowd. Absolutely everything stops.

"Remain calm." A voice slices through the silence. It's Webber.

Dull gray spotlights roar to life above us. The security guards walk out holding lit candelabras, the flames casting creepy shadows on their angel masks. They place the candles on all the tables, then proceed to light the old lanterns on the brick walls. It's like they knew this was going to happen.

This must be what Webber meant when he said they were "the prepared ones."

"Ooh," someone nearby says. "Mood lighting."

As my eyes adjust to the faded light, a figure steps onto the stage.

"Everything is fine," Dean Webber says. "There has been a blackout across the city. Luckily, the factory was designed for emergencies like this. You'll see the generator has kicked in, and in a few minutes everything will be back up and running, albeit a little slower. For the safety of all concerned, we are locking down the building. No one is to leave or enter."

As though waiting for his signal, the guards push closed the wide double doors that lead out onto the street. Automatic bolts slide into place, locking us all inside. Black screens slide down over the windows.

Alarm bells ring inside me. This isn't just some renovated sewing factory or high-class event space, it's a goddamn dystopian fortress.

And now we're all trapped inside it with a leader who has dark plans for us. I know for a fact that he is willing to kill anyone who tries to stop him.

CHAPTER TWELVE

T his is when we panic." Frank gulps hard. "Right?"

The music starts blaring again, like the dean is trying to hype up the student body into a sense of normalcy—and it's working. They get back to dancing the night away. But after what I've seen tonight, I know there's absolutely nothing normal about any of this.

"What the . . . ?" Frank says, looking at his Apple Watch. The screen flashes on and off, and he taps it. "Ugh. My watch is glitching."

"How did you get that past the guards?"

Frank adjusts his collar. "Pari isn't the only one with skills. That goon was too busy muttering orders into his old-school walkie-talkie to notice my watch was still on. Who uses those dollar-store walkies, anyway? Dean Webber can afford those high-tech earbuds or James Bond–style nanotech devices, and he's got his guys using battery-operated bricks."

I tug on his sleeve. "Frank. Focus."

He shakes off his rant. "Sorry." He looks down at his watch, and then his gaze snaps back to mine. "Wait! Pari has her phone, right?"

I nod. "Yeah. She's got way too much sensitive fanfic on there to give it up at the door like we did."

He taps something on his watch, then holds it up to his mouth. "Where are you?" Then he taps the screen again. "Okay. Just texted her."

Well, that was easy.

But then Frank taps his watch again, his brow pinched together. "It says it wasn't delivered." He tries to open different apps on his watch, but it's not cooperating. "That's weird. Blackouts don't usually affect cell phone towers, do they?"

I shrug. "How the hell should I know? Maybe the cell towers are overloaded from everyone in the city trying to call each other because of the blackout."

"I'll try Find My Phone," Frank says. He opens the app, and the little red pin pops up. It shows that the phones are being stored in the building, but all the way on the other side. His screen glitches again, and the app shuts down.

I think of my parents and hope this blackout doesn't reach across the river to Queens. They'll be so worried about me. Shit. I need to get to my phone, let them know I'm okay. They think I'm tutoring on the Upper West Side. My mom can't handle this kind of stress. It will cause her chronic pain to flare up even more than it already has been.

"If we can get to our phones," I think out loud, "we can call Pari and find out where she is."

Frank nods. "Yeah, but how do we—?"

"Give me your watch."

He cocks his head, but does what I asked and hands me his watch. Then I take it over to the nearest guard.

"Excuse me, sir?" I say in my best helpless-little-girl voice. "I found this smart watch, and I know these are supposed to be locked away so I thought I'd better give it to you."

The guard nods, takes the watch, and turns on his heels like a soldier. Frank and I watch as he moves through the crowd, then slips through an unmarked door.

"Let's go," I say.

I take Frank's hand and start pulling him across the dance floor, following the guard. If my plan works, he'll lead us right to our phones.

"Sorry I had to sacrifice your watch," I say before we walk through the door. "I know it was a Christmas present."

Frank shrugs. "We'll get it back. Besides, I'd sacrifice anything for Pari."

We push the door open and peek through. The guard hurries toward a stairwell at the end of a gray hall. I let him get a few steps up before we follow. Frank and I stay ten feet behind him for the next five minutes, twisting our way through the factory. By the time the guard stops at another door, we must've gone up three sets of stairs and walked down half a dozen hallways.

A crackling sound rips through the air, and I cover my ears until it stops. It's the guard's walkie-talkie.

"Listen up," a voice says through the speaker. It's Mason.

"Keep this quiet, but we got a high-risk individual in the building. Suspect is female, wearing a red dress and gold mask with, uh, spikes on top. If you see her, apprehend her and bring her to me."

I can't breathe. That's me. The head goon has just sent his whole team of goons after me. Frank takes my hand and tugs on it, but I can't move.

The guard has stopped unlocking the door. He pockets the watch and turns around. And suddenly we are face-to-face with him again, only this time he thinks I'm the bad guy.

"Run!" Frank says as he pulls on my hand, and this time my body moves. We run as fast as we can through the belly of the building, turning right and left and right again until it feels like we're going in circles. We're like rats in a freaking lab experiment.

We're sprinting past a set of three elevators, and I stop and press one of the buttons. A door opens, and I reach inside and press the button for the basement level, then jump out again. Then Frank and I wait around a corner and hope the guard falls for my plan. My lungs burn. I don't know how much more running I can do.

The guard skids to a stop at the elevators, checks the digital display that reads B↓, then presses the call button.

"Suspect is headed to the basement level," he says into his walkie-talkie.

The guard gets into the elevator, the doors close, and I slide to the floor.

"This is bad," I whisper, forcing down the lump in my throat.

Frank sits down next to me. "It's not ideal."

Deep breaths, Waverly. Remember those therapy memes you've seen on Instagram. In and out. In ... and ... out. But it's hard to breathe deeply when every awful thing I've seen tonight is fighting for the main stage in my mind. I can't sit still. I need to keep moving.

Frank sits up straight, tilting his head to the side. "Do you hear that?"

It takes me a second, but I swear I hear screams. Terrified, bloodcurdling screams.

We get up and follow the sounds down to the end of the hall, where a round stained-glass window sits high up, close to the ceiling. Even with all the main windows of the building shuttered closed, this one is cracked open an inch, enough for the outside world to seep in. I look around for something to stand on—a bench, box, whatever—but the halls are empty of furniture.

"Here," Frank says as he lowers himself down. "Jump on. I'll lift you up so you can see outside."

I hesitate, look down at my wide, flowing dress, then back at him. As curious as I am to find out what's happening out there, the idea of doing it while Frank's head is between my thighs is unappealing, to say the least.

As though reading my mind, he gives me a wounded look. "I'll keep my eyes closed the whole time."

"And your hands to yourself," I add.

"And my hands to myself." He shoves them in his pockets but has to pull them out again to keep his balance while he squats down lower to the floor. "Climb aboard!"

I chew on my bottom lip in concentration as I bunch the skirt of my dress up. "No peeking," I remind him as I awkwardly lift one leg over his shoulder, then another. My dress is too heavy to hold behind his head, so it falls right over his face.

"Uhh," he says from under me. "I literally can't see a thing."

"Good," I say, then pat him on the shoulder. "Giddy-up, then."

I straighten my back in an attempt to keep my balance as Frank slowly stands to his feet.

"We need to move closer," I say. "Take a step forward."

He does as I ask, and I'm able to take hold of the windowsill to keep us stable. Sitting on Frank's shoulders, I'm the perfect height to see through the window. I push it open as far as it can go, but the moment I peer out, I regret it.

The first thing I notice is the sky. It's changing colors right before my eyes. Blue, purple, green, orange, red, like aurora borealis on speed. With the electricity out, the rainbow-hued ether is the only thing illuminating the city, touching the buildings, streets, and bridges with its soft glow. The scattered clouds roll like ocean waves, ebbing and flowing, electric ripples over the East River.

On any other night in Manhattan, you're lucky to see a handful of stars shining through the light pollution, but now they crowd the sky like thousands of tiny pinholes. I can count at least a dozen planes circling in the air over Manhattan, much more than normal on any other night. If the blackout has reached LaGuardia Airport or JFK, then landing would be near impossible for them. And since both airports are in Queens, if they're blacked out, that means my parents are in the dark, too.

I stare up at it all with beautiful terror. And then I turn my attention to the streets below, and my fear only grows. I can see the FDR Drive, cars idling bumper-to-bumper, the stranded passengers getting out to watch the sky. At the intersection on the corner, the electrical box is on fire. Hundreds of people gather on the sidewalks, some wandering like they're lost, some staring up slack-jawed at the wavelike sky, others running like their lives are in danger. Smoke rises from manholes and the grates looking down into the subway. A car drives through the intersection and immediately slams into another, a result of the malfunctioning traffic lights. The sound of metal twisting and people screaming echoes off the dark buildings. Sirens fill the air, but the police cars speed right past the accident, like there's something even more serious to attend to.

"What do you see?" Frank asks from inside my skirt.

I open my mouth to answer, but words fail me. How do I even begin to describe it?

"It's . . ." The pit in my stomach threatens to swallow me whole. It could be a nuclear attack, the start of World War III, the end of the world. And I'm at a party, separated from my mom and dad. I've never felt more afraid. "This isn't just a blackout, Frank."

He shifts his weight underneath me, making me clutch the windowsill so tight my knuckles turn white. "What do you mean?"

"Something big has happened," I say. "The sky is on fire. Everything is on fire."

Frank taps my leg. "I'm putting you down now. I need to see." He slowly lowers himself until he's kneeling on the floor, and I climb off him with wobbly legs. Everything feels off, wrong, like the Earth has tipped on its axis and reality is slipping. Once I'm down, Frank backs up, then runs toward the window. In an impressive show of athleticism, the kind I've never seen from him before, he kicks himself up the wall and grabs hold of the windowsill. Then he pulls himself up to look outside.

"What the fuck," Frank says, his voice cracking. "It's like *The Purge* out there. And what the hell is up with the sky?!"

"Right?" I reply, my own voice not sounding so stable either. "I'm telling you, this is more than just a blackout. Maybe a meteor hit or Russia hacked the grid or something."

Frank cranes his neck to get a better look at the sky. "Or aliens."

I throw my arms up in the air. "Who knows?" I can't believe I'm actually considering the wild idea that aliens have landed. Maybe I really am just having a really fucked-up nightmare. "This is . . . I can't even process what's happening right now."

Frank's arms finally give way, and he drops to the floor with a thud. As he lies there, the expression on his face changes from shock to concern. "I need to get home. My mom and sister will need me."

"We can't leave—"

"Without Pari." He finishes my thought. "I'm with you, one hundred percent." He climbs to his feet, wipes nonexistent dust off his pants, and adjusts his mask.

We were so close to getting our phones. The guard was literally unlocking the door. Now I don't know where the hell we are. I'm so frustrated I could scream.

"We'll just have to search every room for Pari or our phones, and whichever we find first will help us find the other."

"I swear," he says as we get moving, "after this, I'm never giving my phone to anyone again."

"Same," I say.

"Where the hell are you going?!" a man's voice yells.

Frank and I freeze.

CHAPTER THIRTEEN

We've been over this," an angry voice spits. "You're not allowed up to the Red Room until it's time."

"Ash has been up there!" another voice retorts. It's Jack, fighting with his dear old dad.

Frank and I are sidled up against a wall, listening from around a corner.

"That's because she needed to meet some people," Dr. Bradley says. "But she's in the Palms now. And that's where you should be, too. Keep up appearances a little longer."

Ash. My heart skips a beat. Suddenly I find myself stepping into view, ignoring Frank's feeble attempts to stop me.

Dr. Bradley spots me immediately, and his face lights up. "Caroline! Sweetheart!"

Puke.

He opens his arms wide and walks toward me, pulling me into a shallow hug.

Double puke.

Jack stands behind him, narrowing his eyes at me.

His dad holds me at arm's length, squeezing my shoulders a little too hard. "I'm so very sorry about your father. He's been such a good friend to us, a brother, even." I nod. He goes on. "What are you doing back here? Headed to the Palms with all the other cool kids, huh?"

"Yep," I say. "And looking for Jack." I walk over to Jack and take his hand, then put on my best girlfriend voice. "Where have you been?"

Jack rolls his eyes. "Around."

But Dr. Bradley is distracted by something, and I realize Frank's big shoes are poking out from the corner he's trying to hide behind.

"Oh, that's Frank," I say, laughing, staying casual as possible. "He's coming to the Palms, too. Frank, don't be shy!"

Frank awkwardly steps into view, rubbing the back of his neck sheepishly.

"Frank," Dr. Bradley repeats. "Oh, Francis, isn't it?"

Frank's eyebrows rise, but he nods.

Bradley smiles like the Cheshire Cat. "I've heard some very promising things about you, young man. Quite the scientific mind you have."

Frank nods again.

"Not much of a talker, though, I see?" Bradley laughs and playfully punches Frank on the shoulder. "Well, I'm sure that'll change once we get to know each other. We'll have plenty of time to do that!"

Jack clears his throat. "Dad."

Something shifts in Bradley's eyes. A realization, maybe? "Right. All in good time. Anyway, you kids go and have some fun! I'll see you at midnight."

"What happens at midnight?" I ask.

"Dean Webber's midnight toast, of course." He pats Jack on the back, then walks away.

As soon as he's gone, I let go of Jack's hand and start walking. Jack follows.

"Um, where are you going?" he asks.

"The Palms, obviously," I say confidently.

"Right," he says, with a smile in his voice. "But it's the opposite direction. Don't you remember, Caroline?"

Shit. Why did I have to get confident?

Frank and I follow Jack to the Palms, which turns out to be a private lounge decorated in a tropical theme. Real palms, ferns, and plants like birds-of-paradise adorn the whole room, while the walls and floors follow a leafy green-and-pink pattern. Yellow and green velvet chairs and couches sit low to the floor around glass tables, and a bar serves fruity cocktails. To my relief, there are zero guards here, but on the downside it's filled with the people who hate me most: Lance, Alice, and all of Caroline's one-percent crew. It's a good thing they think I'm her; otherwise Frank and I would be dead meat.

Ash is sitting on a couch away from everyone else, nursing a drink with a lime in it.

"I would like to point out that A, this was not part of our

plan," Frank mutters in my ear, "and B, this is a very, very bad idea."

"I don't disagree," I say. "I just—I just need to talk to Ash and then we can get back to our plan. I'm really sorry."

I've already missed too many chances to talk to her tonight; I need to take this one while I have it. Alice tries to talk to me, calling me Caroline and saying fake nice things about Gregory, but I can't even, so I ignore her and make a beeline for Ash.

"Ash," I say, standing over her.

"Waverly," she replies, without looking up. My legs shake, and I sit down on the coffee table across from her.

"How did you—" I try to ask, but she talks first.

"We don't have much time," she says. "I wanted to call you. But I couldn't." She glances over to the bartender, then at me. Our eyes lock. "They wouldn't let me. He wouldn't let me."

"Who?" I don't know why I ask that. I already know the answer. I shake my head. "Why? How?" Ugh. All the questions I've wanted to ask her for months are tumbling out in a mess. Reality hits me like a punch in the gut; I'm actually talking to Ash again. I've imagined how this would go down countless times. I've rehearsed the speeches I'd give her, detailing the betrayal I felt when she ghosted me. I'd written and rewritten scripts of how this would play out, and in my head I was always bold and strong and well-spoken. But right now I'm like putty in her hands, and all I want is for her to tell me it was all a horrible mistake. I want to hear her say she loves me one more time.

She leans in closer. "He's probably watching right now. He made me leave New York, Waverly. He'd had his people following me forever, and I had no idea. That's how he found out about us. He didn't want me with you. He doesn't approve of you and me. He said that's not my destiny. That I'm supposed to lead in the new world. I thought he wanted what was best for me, for all of us. But he only cares about himself. It's happening tonight, Waverly. Soon."

I reach out and take her hand, and it feels just like I remember. "Listen, I know something big happened outside. More than a blackout. Frank and I, we're gonna find Pari and get outta here. Come with us. We'll protect you."

Her eyes well with tears. "You have no idea what's coming, or what he's capable of."

I want to believe her. I want to trust that everything she's telling me is true, that she's a victim in all this, that she never wanted to leave me. But I'm afraid. And it's not just my heart on the line this time, it's my life, and the lives of my friends.

"I know he had Jeff Ramsey killed tonight. And that you were there."

She pulls her hand out of mine. There's a tense silence. "So you know what he's really like. And you should know that you can't save me."

A voice shatters our bubble.

"Caroline!" Max calls from the entrance. "You disappeared!"

Ash slides away, putting some distance between us, and leaving me more confused than ever. But people are watching, so

I snap back into Caroline mode. "Yeah. The party was too much."

Max frowns as she gets closer, bypassing everyone else in the lounge to get to me. She has genuine concern in her eyes, and I feel like such a jerk.

"Can I talk to you?" she says. "In private."

Ash stands up and downs her drink. "I was just going to the bar anyway."

I want to stop her, but I don't know how to do it without blowing my cover, so I let her leave and then turn to Max. She takes both my hands in hers, and sucks in a deep breath.

"You know you're my best friend, right?" she asks.

"Of course," I reply.

"And you know I'd never lie to you," she adds.

I swallow the lump of guilt in my throat and nod.

Max leans in. "I know you've already got way too much going on, but you need to hear this: Jack can't be trusted. He's cheating on you."

Okay, Waverly. Pretend to be shocked. "Wait. What? How do you know that?" I sniffle a little, for extra effect. It's not going to earn me an Oscar nom, but it works.

"I saw him. Tonight. Kissing a girl." Max looks around like she's expecting to see the girl, then turns back to me. "I didn't recognize her, because her mask covered her whole face. But she was wearing an emerald gown."

The girl in the green dress strikes again. First I see her getting all up in Ash's face, then Max sees her making out with Jack. Who the hell is she?

Jack must hear his name being thrown around, because he wanders over to us with a beer in his hand. "Max, you're looking lovely this evening."

Max shoots daggers at him. "Don't even."

Jack flashes his pearly whites. "What did I do this time?"

Max turns to me expectantly, and I realize I'm going to have to play the scorned girlfriend. And it has to be an A+ performance.

I spring to my feet. "Uh, you know exactly what you did, you asshole!"

Jack's eyes widen. "Excuse me?"

"Max told me everything! You've been cheating on me! Who is she!" I poke him in the chest. "Huh?" Turns out all those hours watching straight romance movies has prepared me for this dramatic reenactment. Everyone, including Lance, Alice, Ash, and Frank, is completely absorbed in the scene playing out in front of them. And then something occurs to me: I might be able to get some information out of this. "Who's the girl in the green dress?"

Jack backs away, so he's facing everyone in the lounge. "You know what? I'm more interested in who the girl in the red dress is."

All eyes turn on me. Fuck.

"What do you mean, Jackass?" Max asks, standing up to join my side. "She's Caroline. Your girlfriend. Or have you forgotten?"

Sweat prickles down the back of my neck.

Jack takes a sip of his drink, then places it back on the bar.

"I know who my girlfriend is. And that girl?" He points to me, raising an eyebrow. "That girl is not Caroline."

Alice rolls her eyes. "Jack, you're drunk."

"You're kinda being a dick, man," Lance says. "Caroline's dad is in a coma, and you're running around kissing other girls and accusing her of being someone else?"

I sink further into shame like it's quicksand. My body won't move; words escape me.

"Shut up, Lance," Jack grunts. "You don't know anything."

Lance shoots up like he's been hungry for a fight. "You really think that, don't you? You think you're the only one who knows what's going down here tonight?"

Jack shoves him back, and then it's game on. Lance takes a swing at Jack and gets him on the jaw. Jack barrels into Lance, and they go flying onto one of the glass tables, shattering it. Alice screams, begging them to stop.

The bartender rushes over and pulls Jack off of Lance. I look around for Ash, but she's just sitting in the corner, seemingly unfazed by any of this.

"Hey!" Jack shouts. He shakes off the bartender. "Where are you going?"

He pushes past Lance and Alice and stomps toward me. Frank steps in his way to protect me, but Jack just laughs and pushes him aside.

"Take your mask off," he orders. Pieces of glass shimmer in his hair.

"Get away from me," I say, but my voice shakes.

In one quick movement, he reaches for my mask. I jerk

away, but his fingertips catch on the jawline of the mask and lift it just enough that I can't see. Before I can fix it he tries again, this time pulling it clear off my face.

Gasps fill the room.

Max gives me a look of pure disgust and steps back, like I'm contagious. "Waverly?"

"I-I'm sorry" is all I can say.

Alice clutches her chest. "What have you done with Caroline?"

It takes me a second to understand what she's asking. Frank has to answer for me.

"She didn't do anything to Caroline," he says, coming to my defense. "Tell them, Waverly."

But I can't. The way they're all looking at me, like I'm a cockroach that scrambled into their dinner party, I just want to run and hide.

"Wow, Waverly," Alice continues, her cold blue eyes piercing through me. "It was obvious you were desperate to be Caroline's friend, but I never thought you were desperate enough to try to *be her*. You're sick!"

I want to call out to Ash, *You know me. You know I'm not a liar.* But she won't even look my way.

I turn to Max instead. "I didn't steal Caroline's identity. This was her idea."

Alice pushes past me. "I'm getting security."

"No!" I beg her. "Please, don't!" But she's already marching off to the guards.

Ash doesn't defend me. Max doesn't look at me. Lance laughs. All my biggest fears of being humiliated and revealed as a fake have come true, with the added sting of Ash's rejection on top. Tears well in my eyes. I pick up my mask, take Frank's hand, and head for the door.

A hand grabs me by the elbow and swings me back around. Jack snarls at me.

"You're not going anywhere."

I try to wrestle out of his grip, but Jack is stronger than me. Then, out of nowhere, Frank's fist connects with Jack's face, knocking him back enough that he lets me go.

Another fight breaks out, this time between Jack and Frank. I've never seen Frank like this—eyes wild, jaw tight, fists curled in front of him like he's done this before. Jack throws a punch and Frank dodges it like a pro, then follows with a swift hit in the ribs that makes Jack double over. Max tries to break it up, while Lance just sits at the bar, enjoying the show. Ash has her head buried in her hands in the corner. I don't know what to do.

I hear the sound of high heels behind me, and there's Alice returning with the cavalry, led by Mason. I feel the blood drain from my face.

The guards break up the fight, taking Jack and Frank by the arms. Another guard puts his hand on Max's shoulder and she shoves him off.

"Don't touch me!" she yells. "I was the one trying to break it up!" He doesn't seem to care, and takes her by the wrists despite her protests. Mason grabs me around the waist and I officially go into freeze mode: my arms and legs grow taut, my stomach tightens, I stop breathing. I am pure fucking panic.

Ash looks up at me as I'm being carried out by the man we both saw commit murder tonight.

"Ash!" I call out to her. "Help us! You can stop this!"

She stands up and takes a step forward. But then she stops. She does nothing.

Mason laughs at me. "She ain't gonna help you! She's one of us."

He carries me down the hall, and Ash appears in the doorway. I try one more time. "Ash. You don't have to be one of them. Please. I came here for you. I'm here for you."

Mason laughs harder.

Someone pulls Ash back into the Palms room.

The door slams shut.

She's gone.

CHAPTER FOURTEEN

According to Google Maps, I have arrived at my destination. I peek out from under my black umbrella, squinting through the light rainfall, and frown.

This doesn't look anything like a tennis court.

The building before me is an old brown brick structure, dating back to 1900 according to the cornerstone, with stone arches over the dark windows and doors. The placard on top says THE HEIGHTS CLUB, so it has to be the place.

I made the arduous subway journey from Sunnyside to Brooklyn Heights this rainy Saturday morning for a very special reason: it's my girlfriend's eighteenth birthday. Ash's schedule is so packed that she's not having a party or dinner or doing anything to celebrate until after graduation, so I've decided to surprise her by showing up to her tennis match with her present.

It's not much—what do you get the girl who has everything?—but I know she'll love it. One of Ash's hobbies is collecting different editions of her favorite book, *The Great Gatsby*. I admit, when she first told me that she rereads the F. Scott Fitzgerald classic every Christmas, I judged her a little for it. The chip on my shoulder revealed itself and I found myself harping on about how so many of the rich kids at my school were obsessed with that story, but completely ignored its lessons. It wasn't until after I'd finished my rant that she told me why it was important to her.

In 1934, her maternal great-grandmother, Rose, worked as a switchboard operator at the Plaza Hotel, where F. Scott Fitzgerald and his wife, Zelda, often stayed. Rose saved her pennies and bought a copy of *The Great Gatsby*, and asked him to inscribe it for her.

"It says, 'For Rose, on a snowy New York day in February. F. Scott Fitzgerald.'" I remember Ash's gaze seeming far away when she recited the words. "Rose gave it to my nonna, my nonna gave it to my mother, and now it's stored in a temperature-controlled lockbox in a bank downtown. My mom showed it to me when I was little, when it was still just in our family library. You'd love it, Waverly," she had told me. "The royal-blue cover, gold spine. A true Roaring Twenties relic. It's worth around forty thousand dollars, but to me and my mom, it's priceless."

My heart still aches just remembering that conversation. I'd fully insulted her dead mom's most cherished item. But today, I'm here on her birthday, and I have a gift that will make up for that—and then some. It's a cross-stitch of the cover of the 1934 edition of *The Great Gatsby,* the one her great-grandmother had inscribed. I stitched it myself in my spare time over the last month. Now, even though the original is locked away, she'll be reminded of it every day.

I fold up my umbrella and shake off the raindrops, and some of my nerves while I'm at it. Her dad and some friends from school are here today, too, but I'm going to keep a low profile and sit at the back. If anyone asks, I'll just say I have a tennis lesson or something.

I walk up the steps and try to open the glass door, but it won't budge. I try pushing it instead (I'm prone to pulling a push-only door and vice versa), but still, nothing.

A white woman with dark hair pulled into a tight ponytail appears by my side. She's carrying a squash racket and wearing an all-white Lululemon outfit. I step aside as she swipes a dark green card into a slot on the door. Like magic, it opens for her and she steps inside. I prop the door open with my foot, wait until she's through another set of doors, then walk in.

The foyer is all marble and minimalism. Two smiling white women watch me from behind the front desk, under big gold lettering that says THE HEIGHTS CLUB.

"Can I help you?" one of them asks, drawing out the word "you."

I'm starting to think this isn't like the tennis courts at the park near my house. This is like a legit club. I straighten my shoulders and try to act like I'm supposed to be here.

"I'm just here to watch a tennis match," I say. "My friend is playing."

Her teeth disappear, but the smile remains. "Mhmm. Are you a member with us?"

Crap. "Oh. Uh. I didn't realize I needed to be a member just to—"

"Did your friend fill out a guest pass for you?" She says "friend" with invisible air quotes. My blood pressure rises.

"No, I wanted to surprise her."

Suddenly, she's out from behind the desk and giving me a walk-and-talk back toward the door. "I'm so sorry, we're a members-only club. Next time, be sure to have your friend provide you with a guest pass prior to your arrival, okey dokey?"

And I'm back outside.

The match will be starting any minute, so I shoot off a quick text to Ash.

> surprise! i'm outside! i came to give you your bday present
> and cheer you on but i didnt realize it was members
> only :/

Rain starts to fall heavier, so I flip open my umbrella and wait. But a reply never comes. I distract myself with an audiobook from my library app for the next two hours, convincing myself it'll be worth it to see her face when she opens her present.

The doors of the club open, and there she is. Her cheeks are flushed, glowing from the game, and she's grinning from ear to ear. She must have won. Alice and Max step out behind her, patting her on the shoulder. Then there's Dean Webber, beaming. Ash pulls her phone out of her gym bag and checks it. Her smile changes.

I fix my damp hair and get my own smile ready. Ash looks around, and we lock eyes. I wave with the hand holding her gift bag.

Ash turns and walks away, leading her friends to the Webbers' town car. Her dad follows. No one even notices I'm there. I watch as the car pulls onto the street and drives away. My phone buzzes with a text.

I'm sorry. Talk later.

I cry on the subway, catching my pathetic reflection in the windows every now and then. Hair and clothes rain soaked. Eyes and nose red from tears. Birthday gift in my lap.

Was she embarrassed? Ashamed? Afraid that my just being there would out her? Or is it more than that? Maybe it has nothing to do with the fact that I'm out, and everything to do with the fact that I'm not *in*—not in her class, her friend group, her preppy private tennis club.

Or maybe it's because I'm autistic. She's afraid of being associated with the girl who needs extra time on tests and carries fidget toys with her to class and visits the school counselor every week for help with anxiety. It doesn't matter that I worked hard enough to score a scholarship or that one day I'll be in the same income bracket as all of them. I'm branded.

Or, hell, maybe it's all three, and I'm triple fucked.

CHAPTER FIFTEEN

D on't you know who I am?" Jack growls at the guards as they drag us all through the factory. "My father will—"

Mason scoffs. "Your father will thank me for this when the time comes." Finally, he puts me back on the floor, but doesn't release me from his grip, his sausage fingers digging into the back of my neck. I'm trying as hard as I can to be brave, but all I can think about is how much I want my mom. For the first time in all this mess, it's hitting me that I might never see her or my dad again.

A door creaks open and Mason pushes us all into a small room. It doesn't have any of the style or character of the rest of the rooms—there's no theme or aim to impress here. It's just a box with white walls, a couch and a couple of wooden kitchen chairs, a red rug in the middle, and a lonely light bulb hanging from the ceiling.

But there's one incredible difference between this room and the others.

Pari is stretched out on the couch, arms behind her head, sleeping. "Pari!"

Her eyes snap open at the sound of my voice. "Thank fuck!" She sits up, grinning from ear to ear, and we hug so tight I can hardly breathe, but I don't care.

"What are you all doing here?" Pari asks, looking at all of us.

"We came to rescue you," Frank says as he helps Pari to her feet and hands her her cane.

Mason slams the door shut and locks it from the outside, making us all jump.

She puts a hand on Frank's shoulder and says, deadpan, "Good job."

Jack bangs on the locked door. "You'll regret this! When my dad hears, your membership will be revoked!"

Membership? What, is he threatening to take the Heights Club away? I doubt that will make Mason race back here and let us go. Doesn't really seem like a tennis or squash kind of guy.

Pari purses her lips into a hard line. "You tell 'em, Jack. Nothing scarier to an ex-cop on a power trip than a little boy telling his daddy on him."

God, I've missed her. Now that we've been reunited, we just need to find a way out of this escape room from hell.

"How do you know he's an ex-cop?" Max asks.

"I've been eavesdropping," she replies. "When he's not bullying teenagers, he's blabbing on his walkie-talkie or bragging endlessly to other guards about how Webber plucked him from the force and offered him this 'sweet job'"—she does air quotes—"and how it's scored him and his family all-inclusive tickets to some secret-society bullshit."

Jack dumps his mask on a nearby couch. "Well, I don't care who he is. He has no right. I'm still a lot higher than him on the food chain." Then he goes back to banging his fists on the door like an angry gorilla at the zoo.

Frank runs his hands through his hair. "Jack, will you shut the hell up? You're not helping."

"You wanna go again, bud?" Jack taunts, jutting out his chin.

I stand between them. "Can we cool it with the toxic-masculinity contest, guys? We don't have time for this."

"What do you mean 'we'?" Max asks me. "None of us would even be locked up in here if it weren't for you and your little charade."

She's not wrong. "I'm really sorry, Max. I never meant for it to go this far. None of this was part of the plan."

She crosses her arms over her chest. "And just what was your plan? Steal Caroline's identity while she sits by her father's hospital bed? To what end, Waverly?"

Everything I want to say overwhelms me. I take in a deep breath, and choose my words slowly. "I didn't steal anything. Caroline didn't want to come to the masquerade. She offered me her dress, her mask, to go in her place."

Pari nods. "She's telling the truth. This whole thing was Caroline's idea."

Max raises an eyebrow incredulously. "I find it hard to believe Caroline would let you run around pretending to be her. She has a reputation to uphold."

Ouch. That one stings. Frank shakes his head at her, and I can tell from the look in his eyes that his insecurities about being a scholarship kid were just hit, too. We know we're different. We don't need the constant reminders.

"I'm so sick of all you spoiled assholes," he snaps, sneaking a glare at Jack. "The world is basically ending outside, and you and your families are here partying, living it up. Meanwhile, my family and Waverly's family are out there probably worried sick about us, and we're locked in here with you."

"What are you talking about?" Max asks. "What's happening outside?"

Before Frank can explain more, Jack marches over to him, sticking a finger in his face. "Who are you calling an asshole? You're the assholes! Walking around like you're so much better than everyone else because you're some kind of geniuses. You have no idea how hard it is to be me."

I'm genuinely surprised that he sees us like that. I mean, yeah, Frank is a literal genius, but I'm not even close. I just work really fucking hard. But I'm not at all shocked that he sees himself as some kind of victim. Pari bursts out laughing.

"Yeah," she says to Jack. "Whatever you say, Your Highness. No one's buying your poor-little-rich-boy act."

Max huffs out a frustrated breath. "Seriously. What the

fuck is going on? Where is Caroline? Why are you saying the world is ending?"

"Caroline is probably at the hospital," I say. "With her dad. But we organized this whole Princess Swap thing before he . . . before his accident. She said she was sick of parties, tired of performing for everyone all the time, and she wanted a night off. And after being her for a few hours, I can't say I blame her. Being Caroline is fucking exhausting."

Max nods. "I can relate to that."

Frank sighs. "And, okay, we don't know *for sure* that the world is ending. But the sky is on fire and the power has gone out all over the city. Waverly and I caught a glimpse through an open window."

"It was chaos," I say. "Cars crashing into each other, people running around, shit exploding."

Jack stretches out on the couch. "Sounds like we're in the safest building in the city, then, huh?"

"Listen," I start. "There's something else you should know. Earlier tonight, I saw Mason murder Jeff Ramsey."

Max holds her hands up and closes her eyes. "Wait. You saw *what*?"

"I saw Mason, the ex-cop turned head henchman, kill Jeff Ramsey. With a fire poker. In the cigar room."

Jack scoffs. "Yeah. And I saw Max kill Congressman George in the library with a candlestick."

"Shut up!" I snap. God, he's so irritating. "Webber was right there, he let it happen. Hell, he probably would have done it himself if Mason hadn't stepped in first. It happened right in front of his whole gentleman's club of supervillains. And I'm pretty sure Webber had something to do with Gregory's coma."

"Get real." Jack rolls his eyes. "You listen to too many true crime podcasts."

"Why would I lie about this?" I ask.

I know I should mention that Ash was in the room, too, but I can't. Even after her betrayals, there's a piece of me that can't let go. In my heart, I want to believe that she's good, that she's just as much a prisoner in all this as we are right now.

The group sits in stunned silence, and I keep going. "Jeff was arguing with them, saying that Gregory was right. And Webber talked about some woman, Cassandra, and how they need to go ahead with a plan to 'cleanse the world.'"

"This is some Illuminati shit," Pari says.

"White-supremacist shit," adds Max.

"More like *bull*shit," Jack says. "I'm not buying it."

I'm not surprised he doesn't believe me. "Your dad was right there beside Webber when it happened. Maybe he'll tell you all about it on your yacht once all this is over."

Suddenly, Max springs to her feet, pointing at Jack. "What the hell do you know, Jack? Your dad is super tight with Webber, and Gregory, too. Then I see you with this random girl tonight. Stop messing around and tell us what you know!"

We all turn to look at Jack. He stares right back at us, his lips pressed into a hard line. It's like he's trying to figure out how much he wants to tell us—or come up with the perfect lie to throw us off his scent.

"Is she . . ." I start, attempting to put pieces of the puzzle together as I go, "the girl in the green dress, is she Cassandra?"

And then Jack laughs. He actually, for real, laughs. I resist the urge to pounce on him and throw punches until my knuckles bleed.

"Which part of any of this is funny to you?"

The group turns on him, hurling insults and questions and accusations and then even more insults. Finally, he holds his palms up in surrender.

"Okay, okay!" he says. "Jesus Christ. The girl in green is just some girl. I was drunk. Hell, I'm still drunk. Everything with Caroline's dad freaked me out, you know? So I saw a cute girl and we made out for like, a second. Big deal."

I try to burn him with my eyes. "You are such a selfish dick."

He lets his head fall back and lets out a sigh. "You have no idea." It's like even he's exhausted by his own dickish behavior. But even if he is, that means nothing if he does nothing to rectify it. He gets zero sympathy from me.

Jack stands up and kicks one of the wooden chairs over. "I can't believe I'm stuck in here with you losers when I should be getting wasted in the Red Room."

"What's the Red Room?" I ask, remembering the name coming up in the fight he was having with his dad earlier.

"Webber's *private* party room," he says. "Only the biggest names make it inside. My dad spends so much time in that room, it should be named after him. That's where I was supposed to be tonight, but I keep getting relegated to the lower levels like some nobody."

I let out a groan. "I can't believe you're whining about missing the party. We need to get the fuck out of this factory!"

"For your information," he says, fully smug, "the Red Room is your best bet at getting out. It's the only part of the building that isn't affected by the lockdown. There's stairs to the roof and a fire escape that leads down to the street."

I fold my arms over my chest. "How do you know that?"

"Please," he says, waving me off. "You know how many of these parties I've been to? I've been sneaking onto that roof to smoke weed since I was fourteen."

"So you're saying the only way out of this hellscape is through the lion's den," I say. "Otherwise we're stuck in here waiting to meet our doom."

He snorts. "You're so frigging dramatic. Webber's smart—if there's fire or whatever, the building will automatically unlock itself. Stop freaking out. We're safe in here."

Just then, an ear-piercing alarm fills the room. My hands fly up to cover my ears, and my eyes squeeze themselves shut. I rock back and forth until it stops a few seconds later.

When I open my eyes, Pari is searching under the couch. "Found it!" It's her phone, lit up and vibrating loud. The text on the screen reads:

EMERGENCY ALERT

"I threw it under the couch," she explains. "It was glitching like a little bitch. I thought it died."

Jack runs a hand over his face. "You're not supposed to have that."

We all ignore him and crowd around Pari as she opens the alert notification. These aren't new to us; we've all received Amber Alerts more times than I care to remember, and flood alerts during storm season. But this is already different: no other functions on Pari's phone are working. There's just a black screen with white text.

Incoming message. Please adjust volume.
Incoming message.

More noise comes through, and Pari turns her volume down. It sounds like some kind of communication interference, like radio static.

"This is the emergency broadcast system," a female voice begins. "Please wait for an important message from the president."

The air gets sucked out of the room. My mouth goes dry. None of us say a word. And then the familiar voice of the president fills the airwaves.

"My fellow Americans," he begins. "By now, you are probably aware that we are experiencing a historic blackout. To be sure, this is the kind of event the world has never seen before. And I do mean the world. I've spent the last two hours consulting via radio and face-to-face here at the White House with the best scientific minds on the planet, and what they've told me is concerning, I'll admit. But before I go on, I want to make one thing clear: we will get through this. We can be afraid, but we cannot panic. We must remain the strong and courageous people I have always known us to be."

There's a pause. Static. A rustling. I hold my breath.

"As I mentioned, this is no mere blackout. Our scientists have confirmed that a solar flare has disrupted the Earth's atmosphere. This flare has caused power grids to fail not just here in the United States, but all over the globe. Technology as we know it has changed. Communications devices, transportation such as cars and airplanes, home appliances, everything we've come to rely on, we can no longer turn to. I'm talking to you now not through a television or internet streaming service, but through old-school radio waves that my team have managed to send to as many telecommunications devices as they can, but I know this message won't reach everyone it needs to. Forgive us as we attempt to forge our way through these new, but at the same time old, ways of reaching out to you. This will take some time, but I say again, we will make it through this."

Someone sniffles, and I realize Max is crying beside me. I take her hand, and she lets me. Hearing her cry makes the lump in my throat burn, and I can't hold my tears back anymore either.

"Though the cities of the world are dark, we will not be taken by darkness. Though our skies appear to rain fire, we will not be burned. And though our way of life, the technology we have relied on to connect us, has failed us, we will not fail. You see, we as a nation and as a world have come together before, and we will do it again, tonight. We will come together, we will rebuild. Stay strong, America. Good night."

The lights flicker for the hundredth time tonight, but this time it hits different. The lights are struggling to stay lit, using their last bursts of electricity before disappearing into nothing like everywhere else in the city, the country, the world.

The voices on Pari's phone turn to static, and then silence falls over us once more.

I clutch my stomach. Suddenly this dress feels about five sizes too small, and the air in the room feels thin and sparse. I'm sinking into myself, being swallowed whole by shock and terror.

"This can't be happening," I whisper. "This isn't real."

CHAPTER SIXTEEN

My mask sits on the floor at my feet, looking up at me. I stare into its empty eyes like it's somehow going to give me all the answers I seek.

It's probably only been ten minutes since we heard the president speak, but it may as well be a decade. In my mind, I'm racing through everything I've ever read about solar flares—which isn't much. I vaguely remember something online a few months ago about some scientist in Europe who warned of the sun's growing instability, but it lasted less than twenty-four hours on my news feed and I shrugged it off as another internet conspiracy theory.

Shit. All the weird blackouts that have been happening for weeks. I assumed it was Con Ed cutting our power to hoard it for the wealthier zip codes. Regular, old-fashioned class inequality. Or maybe our old building going on the fritz. But those must have been warning signs of something much worse coming our way.

Okay, Waverly, focus. What do I remember about this stuff?

Solar flares are bursts of energy that explode from the sun.

If they make contact with the Earth's magnetic field, it interferes with technology.

Or in this case, wipes it out completely.

The effects of geomagnetic storms can last for years.

I can't remember how badly it affects transportation. Cars were crashing out there, like they were completely out of control. But planes were still in the air. Both have computer chips in them, right? I mean, basically everything has a microchip in it. But Pari's phone still worked enough to get a radio signal. Maybe it takes time for the full effects of a flare to hit.

I swear I read that events like this are highly unlikely. Like, once-in-three-hundred-years unlikely.

I guess this is the three-hundred-year mark. Ugh. I wish I could just google all this.

But if all this is real, the days of googling are over. Same with the days of social media, television—hell, even the ability to turn a light switch on and off. I'd give anything to be able to open social media right now and doom-scroll until I know what the hell is going on in the outside world.

I run my fingers through my hair, massaging my scalp as though it's going to bring my memories of science classes to the surface.

What if there were other signs that I missed, like the blackouts? There could have been warning signs for months. People must have noticed something.

Webber. He noticed. He and his boys' club knew this was coming. But how?

"Dean Webber had some way of knowing this was going to happen," I say, more to myself than to the others. "Something that no one else had."

"Like what?" Franks asks, and I shrug.

"He contributes to archaeology studies, right?" I piece it together as I talk. "Maybe they found some ancient code. Some kind of knowledge that no one else has. However he found out about it, he's known for a while. Long enough to make plans." I think back to Gregory, panicked on the phone, and Jeff in the cigar room. "This Cassandra person warned them this was coming."

Cassandra. The girl in the green dress. They're both connected to all this. Maybe they're one and the same.

Pari sits up straighter. "Maybe she's a psychic? Some incredibly accurate tarot reader or astrologer."

Jack puts on a high-pitched, Valley Girl voice. "Ohmigod, it's like, totally Mercury in retrograde's fault."

Pari gives him the finger. "Astrology is legit, asshole. Why don't you tell us your theories about how Webber got advance warning?"

Jack shuts up then, which is weird. I wish I could pry him open and find out what he knows, because my gut tells me there's a whole lot he's not telling us.

"Unless Mercury blew up like the Death Star, I don't think it's astrological. Astronomical, more like. Maybe Webber has connections at NASA," Frank says. "Or even the NSA. Cassandra could be some kind of secret agent."

Jack groans. "Next you'll be saying he has a secret back channel to Russian oligarchs, and that's how he got the information."

"I know you're being sarcastic," Max says. "But the dean does have connections in Russia. My mom does some work with the United Nations, and she saw Webber and Caroline's father meeting with Russian diplomats and scientists at one of their summits. I overheard her telling my dad after dinner that night."

Jesus.

"Gregory had something to do with it," I say, thinking out loud. "And he works in tech, right? Like, algorithms and artificial intelligence and all that."

Max nods. "Yes. I remember Caroline saying once that he's been investing in tons of high-tech AI companies and inviting research scientists to their penthouse for dinner that she had to pretend to be interested in."

I pick up my mask and start fiddling with the rods of the crown absentmindedly, the fidgeting helping me think. "What if Cassandra isn't a person? What if she's a machine?"

"Like a time machine?" Max asks.

Frank shrugs. "It looks a helluva lot like *Endgame* outside, so I'd buy that. The sky is freaking out and so is the city."

Jack lets out a loud laugh. "And I suppose you think you're Captain America in all this?"

Frank raises an eyebrow, a rare cockiness in his expression. "I'm the only one here from Brooklyn, just like Cap."

"Webber is totally Thanos," Pari adds.

I resist the urge to throw down all my Captain Marvel knowledge. "Okay, we're getting sidetracked. I meant what if Cassandra is, like, a program?"

Pari nods. "I've heard of this. Silicon Valley has been obsessed with predictive AI tech since forever. Maybe Caroline's dad cracked the code."

"And Webber used that knowledge to start doomsday prepping," I say. "Shit. What if this whole building is some kind of apocalypse bunker?"

Pari shakes her head, worry all over her face. "He wants to be the dictator of some new, fucked-up world. One even more fucked-up than this one."

"So, he killed Jeff Ramsey," Frank starts. "Because Ramsey wanted to warn people. And he tried to kill Gregory for the same reason."

My terror shifts to rage. Who knows how long Webber and his cronies knew this flare was coming? They could have told the whole world. Everyone could have prepared.

But of course they didn't tell anyone. Men like them have done this shit since the dawn of time. Hoard resources—money, power, knowledge—for themselves, screw everyone else. Screw the most marginalized communities, who will inevitably suffer most from this disaster. Screw the sick and disabled folks, who need medicine and ventilators and medical equipment powered by electricity to live. Screw the parents with mouths to feed and no idea what to do next to protect their kids.

I thought Webber cared about all of this. He made it a point to help my family. But we were just props in his performance, helping him uphold his image as a hero.

I think of my mom and dad, stuck at home right now, our apartment dark while the sky is lit like Times Square. Worried about me, terrified of what's going to happen to all of us. All the years they've spent working for Webber, believing him when he called us family, giving him every extra cent they could and doing everything he asked of them. And for what? To be left behind, abandoned to fend for themselves while he handed out VIP invitations guaranteeing safety to his rich friends.

Webber could have done something. He could have used this information, his billions of dollars, his connections to the highest forms of government, to make plans and build new systems that would prepare us, protect us. Instead, he used it to renovate this egregious Lower Manhattan escape-room bunker and throw a lavish party for the people with the deepest pockets and their spawn.

In the end, nothing else—and nobody else—mattered. If I hadn't snuck in here tonight, I'd be out there with my family. Right where he wanted us, if he even thought of us at all when planning this entire thing.

Only rich white men would throw a party at the end of the world.

I let out a fierce growl that comes from somewhere deep within my fiery belly. The gold mask sits on my lap, staring up at me, representing everything I'm not and never will be and, now, never want to be. I want to throw it, slam it against the perfect white walls and watch it shatter into a million pieces. But I can't. Not yet. I might still need it to get the hell out of this place.

"So let me get this straight," Jack says as he starts counting on his fingers. "Our theories are: ancient Greek oracle, astrologer, secret agent, Russian spy, and *robot*. You guys watch too much CNN."

"And you're incredibly chill about all this," I fire back. "Almost like you knew this was going to happen, too."

Just then, the door busts open, and Mason's gigantic shadow fills the room. "Come on," he says, motioning for us to move. "Follow me."

Oh, hell, no. I'm over this dude ordering us around. "Why should we?"

His eyes widen under his mask. "Get up. Now."

None of us move an inch. He storms in and grabs Pari by the elbow.

"Unhand me, Hulk!" she snaps at him.

I stand up and start punching his back. My knuckles crack and sting with pain with each hit, but I don't care. I'm a ball of rage, and there's no way I'm letting him take Pari away from us again.

Max and Frank join the scuffle then. We yell and kick and throw fists. Even Jack tries to swing at Mason, but he misses completely. Then, in one smooth movement that is indeed Hulk-like, Mason throws his arms out by his sides, knocking us all back a few feet. Pari is freed from his grip, but he immediately goes for her again.

"Leave her alone!" Frank yells, then launches himself at Mason. But Mason goes for his Taser gun, points it right at Frank, and shoots. The wires reach out like tentacles, hitting Frank in his chest. His whole body tenses, and then he's falling. His back hits the edge of a wooden chair, and it collapses under the impact. Things crack loudly, and I have a sickening feeling it wasn't just the chair that broke. Frank ends up on the floor, bleeding and shaking violently.

Someone screams, and I realize it's me. Frank's so out of control that he jerks his head into the wall repeatedly. I rush over and try to protect his head, but just touching him for a second sends electric shocks up my arm.

And then everything stops. The Taser stops electrocuting him. Frank doesn't move.

"Frank!" Pari calls. She uses her cane to help her kneel down next to him, then takes him by the shoulders and shakes him.

His eyes flutter. "Pari?"

"I'm here," she says. She takes his hands in hers and tries to get him to look at her. "You're okay. You're okay." But then blood drips from his mouth, and she turns to look up at me. I can tell by the pain in her face that she doesn't believe her own words. I fall to my knees on the other side of him.

"Frank." I push his hair back the way he always does. "You good, bud?"

"Yeah," he mumbles. "I'm good. My head hurts a little."

I reach back to touch the back of his head. It's wet with blood. Pari and I exchange a quick glance, then she sees the blood on my fingers and her face falls.

"We need an ambulance," Pari yells. "A doctor, nurse, someone!"

Max heads for the door, but Mason won't let her leave. "My father is a doctor," Max says. "Let us go get him so he can help."

Mason doesn't move. "He doesn't need a doctor."

"Look at him!" I yell, pointing to the blood running down Frank's neck, staining his crisp white shirt. "He needs help!"

Frank makes a gurgling noise and more blood spills from his lips. His words are jumbled, impossible to understand. His fingers squeeze Pari's and she tries to shush him.

"Just breathe." A tear falls onto her cheek. "Okay? Just keep breathing."

But he falls silent, his chest stops rising, blood keeps spilling.

Jack stands next to Max, staring Mason down. "Listen, bro. You have no idea what you just did. That kid isn't just some skinny geek. Webber specifically chose him. Plucked him from obscurity, some burned-out pizza place in Brooklyn, gave him a scholarship, training, a ticket to the Gateway just like yours. But unlike you, Frank is not expendable. He doesn't even know how smart he is, but Webber had him lined up to basically run the place with Gregory. And seeing as you screwed up the Gregory thing, too, this definitely isn't going to go down well with the 'boss.'"

Max slowly turns to face Jack. "What the hell are you talking about?"

I'm wondering the same thing. Whatever it is, Mason seems to understand, but he doesn't move. "You know it's too late," he says. "It is what it is."

Max and Jack join Pari and me beside Frank, trying to get him to speak or move or blink. Jack reaches for Frank's wrist, checking his pulse, and all the color drains from his face. I blink back my tears, not sure if I'm going to faint or throw up or both.

"He's . . ." Jack gulps. "He's dead."

I touch a trembling hand to Frank's neck, then his wrist. Nothing.

Pari and I collapse into tears over Frank's body. The second person I've seen die tonight, only this feels so much more painful, more real, yet unreal all at once. I can't handle all this. It can't be possible.

He was just here. He was just throwing smart-ass remarks at Jack. He was on the dance floor, towering over everyone. He was running through this factory with me, trying to get out of here to help his family.

Oh, god. His family. His mom and sister. They still haven't recovered from Frank's dad dying and the family restaurant closing only a couple of years ago. They've already lost so much, and now this. It's not fair. Why do good people like Frank's family suffer over and over again while slimeballs like Mason and Webber just keep winning? When do the good guys win?

I feel like I'm falling, drowning, dying right alongside my friend. This is too much.

"That's what happens when you don't do what you're told," Mason grunts. "Come on. The boss wants everyone in the ballroom for his midnight toast."

Rage burns through me. I suck in a deep breath and drag my eyes off of Frank in time to see Pari clutch the broken leg of the armchair, squeezing it so hard her knuckles turn pink.

"You son of a bitch." She springs to her feet and swings it at Mason, cracking him on the side of his head so hard the chair leg snaps.

Mason stares down at her blankly, and I jump in between them, afraid of what he'll do to her. But then, he holds a hand to his head, cradling the spot Pari hit. He takes a step forward and I push him back, which is surprisingly easy. He starts to wobble from side to side. It looks like the hit to his head knocked his equilibrium off, because he can't keep his balance. I step back and pull Pari with me, not wanting to be in his path if he goes down. Max and Jack back up against a wall, palms up like they're ready to push him if he wobbles in their direction.

After a few seconds of confused swaying, his eyes roll back in his head, and he tips over like a tree struck by lightning. The floor shakes with his landing.

Pari's shoulders heave with her shallow breath, and she lets the chair leg drop to the floor beside her. I pull her into a hug, both of us trembling so hard from shock that our teeth chatter. Max picks Pari's cane up from where she left it next to Frank, and hands it to her.

"Good hit," she says. But Pari doesn't seem to hear her.

"He's dead," she whispers. "Frank's dead."

I squeeze my eyes shut and realize I'm not breathing. When I finally remember how to pull air into my lungs, it's shaky and sounds more like a sob. None of this feels real.

I force myself to open my eyes and look at Frank, as though that will somehow snap me out of this heavy haze. Jack paces back and forth like a tiger in a cage.

"We gotta go," Jack says.

No one answers, and he repeats it again. We ignore him.

The lump in my throat feels like it's burning a hole through my skin. My tears sting like acid.

Mason starts to twitch, then groan.

"I'm sorry but we really need to go," Max says gently. Jack stops telling us we have to leave and instead starts literally pushing us out the door. I take Pari's hand, pulling her out of the room and away from Frank's dead body.

"We have to find his mom after all this," Pari says, swiping at her tears. "We have to tell her what happened. That he's a hero."

I nod and squeeze her hand tight. "We will."

CHAPTER SEVENTEEN

W here are we even going?" My eyes are cloudy from tears and my brain feels like Jell-O. I don't know how long Max, Pari, and I have been following Jack around the factory.

"To the ballroom," Jack says gruffly. "If I'm not there for the midnight toast, people will get suspicious. Same goes for you, *Caroline*."

I stop in my tracks. "I don't give a fuck. I want to go home."

"Me, too," Pari says.

"You said there's a way out through that Red Room, right?" I ask Jack. "How do we get there?"

Jack sighs. "The Red Room is on the penthouse level. Only the middle elevator of the three in the elevator bank will take you there. It's the thirteenth floor, but the numbers on the keypad skip thirteen because of some old superstitious crap, so you gotta hit fourteen."

Max hesitates. She looks between me and Jack. "You two

go ahead. My mom and dad are still at the party. I can't leave without them."

"We'll wait for you up there," I say. "We won't leave without you." Max nods, then she and Jack start running toward the ballroom while Pari and I turn around and head toward the elevator banks.

For the first time all night, something goes our way, and we find them in record time. We take the middle elevator right up to the penthouse level.

I brace myself in case I need to blend in with the crowd or hide from guards, but the doors open to an empty floor. Pari and I step out, looking around nervously.

"I can see why they call it the Red Room," Pari says with a soft chuckle.

Same. Literally everything is a deep blood red: the walls, the velvet couches and poufs, the shag carpeting, right down to the tiniest details like candles, framed artwork, cloth napkins and cutlery on the tables. It's obsessive.

"Everyone must be in the ballroom for the toast," I say. I should be relieved—this is the biggest win I've had all night—but my reckless heart is disappointed. This means I'll probably never see Ash again. I'm leaving her behind with her murderous father. But the way she stood by and did nothing while Mason carried me away tonight, maybe that's exactly what she wants me to do. Maybe it's what I need to do.

"Whoa." Pari gasps. She's standing over a long table with some kind of display on it. "Check this shit out!"

I stand on the opposite side of the table and marvel at the

model construction. Half of it is a wide block that stands up to my chest, the surface painted to be desertlike, with tiny granules of sand glued to the top. The other half, I see as I walk over to Pari's side, shows some kind of bunker hiding under the surface. Fifteen levels deep, and most of the levels look like nice apartments with miniature kitchens, bedrooms, and living rooms. The lowest levels seem to have water tanks and machinery, while the highest levels have a gym, indoor vegetable gardens, a classroom, and a hospital.

Something catches my eye on the wall behind the model. "Pari. Look."

A huge map hangs proudly in a gold frame. Cursive above it reads: *The Gateway.*

"Gateway," Pari says. "That's what Mason kept saying he got tickets to."

"And Jack." I swallow hard. "Jack said something about Frank. Webber choosing Frank to help run the Gateway?"

The map shows six bunkers, all of them just like the model on the table. They're in a circle on a huge plot of land—an arrow indicates it's somewhere outside of Fort Worth, Texas.

Pari points to a square on the map. "Look at this." She drags her finger to three other squares near each corner, surrounding the bunkers. "It says these are guard towers. Do you think they're for keeping people out, or keeping them in?"

I shudder. "Both."

I lean in closer, noticing names on each of the bunkers. "President Webber. General George. General Bradley. General Ramsey. General Sinclair."

"They're giving themselves titles," Pari says. "That's a red flag."

Shit. "How many people at the party have no idea that he has this planned for them?"

Pari scratches her head. "I don't get it though. How the hell is he going to get hundreds of people from New York to Texas during a solar flare?"

"I don't know. But I bet he has it all figured out. And the only people who know about this are him, his 'generals,' and now us."

We need to tell people the truth, about the solar flare, the Gateway, all of it. We need to warn them.

Pari sighs. "We have to go back, don't we?"

"Yep."

Pari has a superior sense of direction to mine, so it doesn't take long for us to make our way back to the main ballroom. But we decide to go through the kitchen, in case Mason is on the loose again.

I pull open the heavy steel door, and we're greeted by the noise of plates clanging and champagne bottles popping. Waiters zip around, gathering trays and champagne flutes while chefs put finishing touches on desserts and busboys slide heavy crates filled with dirty pots and pans into industrial dishwashers.

"Hey," one of the chefs yells at us. "Youse ain't allowed in here." He throws a towel over his shoulder and glares at us until we move.

We hurry through, careful not to get in anyone's way.

The chef shakes his head and mutters to himself. "Fuckin' brats think they can just walk into my kitchen."

I almost knock over a waiter as he tries to balance a tray of glassware on one hand. "Sorry." Behind him, I catch a glimpse of security guards dropping something into the flutes.

"Get out!" the chef says as he shoves us forward through the double doors, back into the ballroom.

Pari and I stay close together, keeping close to the wall. I look around the room for Max, and spot her on the opposite side of the ballroom, standing in between her parents. It seems like she's trying to whisper something to them, but they shush her as the crowd grows quiet.

Most of the Webber Academy "family" is here in this room, waiting for the dean's midnight toast: parents, children, Webber Academy faculty and staff, wealthy donors and their families. There are politicians, doctors, scientists; everyone gathered here tonight is the kind of person Webber would want to help him birth a new society, one where he is in total control. That's why he's locked everyone in this factory. He needs all these people. This is his new world.

"Is everyone here?" the dean asks from the stage.

Ash stands a few feet behind him, keeping her head down. Waiters start streaming into the room, the trays of champagne glasses balanced on one hand.

Webber claps his hands together. "Wonderful!" He takes a glass of champagne and holds it high. "Again, I want to thank all of you for joining us here tonight at what will go down in history as an event of epic proportions."

Some people chuckle at that, but they have no idea how right he is.

"I'm so proud of what we here at Webber Academy have built together, and I am beyond excited to see what we will continue to build in the years to come."

I take one of the champagne glasses. What the hell, right? Maybe it'll help settle my wrecked nerves enough for me to make it out of this place without a breakdown. I glance down at my glass, but notice something oddly familiar about the way it fizzles. I squint and hold it up closer to my face, straining to see in the dim lighting. There's something small and round at the very bottom, dissolving into the alcohol, leaving a barely noticeable green hue to the champagne.

It's a pill. That's what the guards were dropping into the glasses in the kitchen.

While Webber keeps giving his speech, a terrifying realization hits me: I've seen those little green pills before. My mom used to take them on her worst flare days, to numb the pain. Dad would give her one with water, then tuck her in under her multiple weighted blankets, slip her ice mask over her eyes, and kiss her good night. She'd be knocked out for at least eight full hours. Except one night when she had it with a glass of red wine, and it took longer to kick in and turned her into more of a zombie—she was awake, but it was like she was sleepwalking.

This has to be how he's going to get everyone to the Gateway. Drug them, then lead them onto buses or a train or something.

"A toast to us!" the dean says. He holds his flute high,

and Ash does the same behind him. She's taken her mask off, and I can see her face is frozen blank, like she's trying not to show any shred of emotion. Webber would never drug his own daughter, but does she know what he is about to do to all these people?

I throw my glass onto the floor and it shatters. People around me jump and stare. "Don't drink it," I start telling people. "It's drugged! Don't drink it!"

Pari looks at me, full of confusion. But then she throws her glass on the floor, too.

People around us give us strange looks; some of them laugh condescendingly and roll their eyes. I don't care—people like them have been looking at me like that my whole life. I speak louder. "He's trying to drug you!"

Webber laughs into the microphone. "Guilty. Champagne has always been my drug of choice." He glances to the side, and Mason appears from behind the stage, hand firmly placed on his Taser again. He starts pushing through the crowd to get to us.

"Now, as I was saying," Webber says. "To us! And to the prosperous future of our family." He downs his drink, and Ash does the same.

The crowd holds up their glasses and repeats what he said, like a brainwashed cult. A waiter walks by, and I slam the tray out of his hands. It crashes to the floor, glasses shattering and champagne spilling. I take off my mask.

"Stop!" I yell at everyone, throwing my hands up in the air. "Don't drink it!"

But it's too late. Some already have. I start slapping glasses out of people's hands. Pari goes in a different direction to slap drinks out of people's hands, too.

Someone tries to grab me, and I jump out of reach. I run over to one of the tables, push the vase of flowers off, and climb up.

"Webber is trying to drug all of you! They put pills in the drinks!"

Masked faces peer up at me, slack-jawed and shocked. Mason and his security team make their way over to me from every direction. I don't have much time. "You can't trust him. A solar flare just knocked the world back to the Stone Age, and he's trying to drug us all into submission!"

On the stage, Webber laughs. It drips out of the speakers, filling the room with his arrogant chuckle, only making my rage burn brighter.

"She's telling the truth!" a voice yells from the other side of the ballroom. It's Max. She turns to her parents. "That's what I've been trying to tell you." She pours her champagne onto the floor, and her parents share a concerned glance, then pour their drinks out, too. I almost cry with relief. Finally, adults who actually believe us.

"I saw him kill Jeff Ramsey tonight," I yell. "He tried to kill Gregory, too. None of us are safe! He wants to take you to a bunker called the Gateway and make himself president!"

That takes him aback, his eyes widening. He pulls his minotaur mask right off to reveal his angry, shocked expression. There's the real monster.

"Get her out of here," he yells. Then, as if he's remembered he has an act to keep up, he recovers. A smile breaks out on his face, and another chuckle ripples out of him. "The poor girl has clearly broken into the champagne long before any of us did."

The audience laughs. Mr. Cameron marches up to the table I'm standing on and stomps his foot like a child.

"Waverly," he says, shaking his head. "What on earth has gotten into you? Get down from there this instant. I'm surprised at you. You're usually such a well-behaved young girl."

I flip him off with both hands. "Maybe that's my problem! I've been too well-behaved! I've gone along with everything Webber says, followed all the rules. Well, not anymore! I'm fucking done!"

Mr. Cameron gasps. "Waverly! I would never expect that kind of talk from you! You've been spending too much time with that Pari."

"Good!" I yell, throwing my arms in the air. "Pari has been the only one with any sense around here for too long. We all need to wake up and see what's really going on!"

"Guards," Webber says into the microphone. "Enough. It's time, anyway. Let the people enjoy the party, while they can."

And just like that, the guards file out through the nearest exit. Mason has retreated to the stage to usher the dean and Ash out after them. Ash keeps looking back at me, and I swear she's calling my name, but I can't hear her over the yelling around me.

The music starts up again. All the doors to the ballroom

close. Max runs over and tries to open one, but it won't move. They've locked us in.

Apparently, the other party guests think this is my fault. One of the parents grabs my ankle and pulls, and I fall onto the surface of the table with a painful thunk.

"How dare you disrespect the dean like this," Lance's mother yells, literally clutching her pearls.

"Get off of her, you vultures!" I hear Pari yelling from somewhere nearby.

"She's telling the truth!" Max says. "Just don't drink the champagne!"

But it's no use—people drink it with such purpose, it's like they're doing it just to spite me now. They'd rather risk drinking poison than disobey their leader or stand against the crowd.

"Hey! Hey!" Pari appears, swatting at the adults surrounding me with her cane. "Get away! You're supposed to be the grown-ups here, remember?"

Max's mom rushes over, one of the twists atop her head falling to the side of her face. "Leave the girl alone!" The parents mutter under their breath and start to back away. I fall onto the floor with my eyes closed, trying to stave off another panic attack.

"Waverly," a new voice says. My eyes open. A hand reaches down to help me up, and I take it. It's the girl in the green dress.

"Who are you?"

"Follow me."

Pari and I follow her into one of the curtained-off booths.

Jack trails behind us. I'm about to complain about how flimsy this hiding place is when the girl stands on the seat, reaches up to the portrait (of Dean Webber on a throne, no less), and pulls at it. It swings open like a door, with a small room on the other side.

"Whoa!" Pari gasps. "Plot twist."

"Shh!" the girl hushes us. "Get in!"

Jack climbs in before any of us, because he obviously doesn't believe in the whole women-and-children-first thing.

"We need to get Max," Pari whispers.

I poke my head out from the curtains, and see her standing with her parents, having what seems to be a very intense conversation. Her arms are waving wildly, and they're frowning at her.

I try to whisper-yell her name, but she'll never hear me over the music. Actually yelling will just attract more unwanted attention our way, and the last thing we need is more angry parents swarming around. I need to get her attention.

"Jack, give me your flask," I say.

His eyebrows shoot up to his hairline. "This isn't the time for you to start drinking."

I shake my hands at him impatiently. "Your flask, Jack!"

He huffs but pulls it out of his jacket pocket and throws it over to me. I catch it and peek back out from the curtains again. One of the bright emergency lights points in my direction just enough that if I hold the metal flask at the right angle, it reflects across the room. Just as I'd hoped.

I turn the flask slightly so the beam of light hits Max on

the side of the face. Her parents notice it first. Then all three of them look my way, and I wave them over.

"Okay, MacGyver," Pari says with a grin.

"Waverly!" Jack scolds me from the tiny room when I throw the flask back at him. "There's not enough room for all of us!"

It doesn't take long for Max's parents to reach the same conclusion once they see our exit plan.

Max's dad pulls her into a hug. "You go. Get out of here. We'll find another way."

Max shakes her head. "No way."

Her mother pushes her through the curtain. "Maxine. Go. We'll be fine."

They stand guard in front of the booth while the rest of us climb through the secret door. Once I'm squished inside with the others, I realize it's not a room, but an old galley elevator, complete with a pull rope.

The girl in green takes hold of the rope. "We all need to work together to do this. Just grab it and pull down."

We do as she asks. My palms sweat and turn red immediately, but we get it working and start lifting ourselves up. Soon, I can tell Pari is hurting. The pain she'll feel from doing something like this will be ten times worse than ours, so I nudge her and give her a nod to let her know she can stop to rest. She does, and a few beats later we all stop.

"We're here," the girl in green says. She pushes the door open and exits first; then we all help Pari climb out second. We step out from behind another oil painting, this time into a cold, stone-walled room filled with shelves and shelves of alcohol. Racks of wine bottles, barrels of who-knows-what, crates of whiskey that go all the way up to the ceiling.

Jack rubs his hands together and grins. "Jackpot!"

"Not now, Jack," the girl in green says as she closes the painting door. Then she turns, huffs out a breath, and pulls off her mask.

CHAPTER EIGHTEEN

Caroline?"

I can't believe I didn't figure it out earlier.

Max throws her arms around her, squeezing her tight. "Are you okay? How's your dad? Did you really sign off on Waverly masquerading as you all night?"

When Max releases her, Caroline says, "I'm okay. Yes, Waverly masquerading as me was my idea. And as for my dad . . ." She swallows. "He hasn't woken up yet, and with the hospitals running on backup generators now, I don't know if he ever will. But he left me something." She pulls a folded piece of paper out of a pocket in her dress. "He knew people were coming for him."

She opens the note and starts reading it aloud.

"Dearest Angel, if you find this, then they've won. I won't ask you to forgive me for knowing what was coming and only preparing for our own survival. I deserve far more than whatever

punishment they will bring my way. Whatever happens, whatever new world you step into, do so as your own woman. Do not let yourself become a follower. And do not trust Owen Webber. Don't make the same mistakes I did. I don't have much time, and anything more I could tell you wouldn't help you and would only cause you more pain. So, I'll finish by saying I am so desperately sorry, and I love you more than life itself."

We all stare in stunned silence. I can't get the image of Gregory in his office out of my mind. I wonder if he'd already written the note by then, or if he sat down at his desk to do it after I left. Caroline refolds the note with care and purpose, like she knows it contains her father's last words. Then she slides it back into her dress, straightens her shoulders, and raises her chin.

"I didn't know what it meant at first," she says. "I still don't, not fully. But I knew I had to dig deeper, find out what was going on. And with Waverly already dressed as me, I could sneak in to investigate unnoticed. I know all of Webber's secret-society passwords, so they let me in, no questions asked." She takes in a deep breath, like the weight of everything is getting to be too much, and I feel awful for her. It turns out that this thing has touched everyone, no matter how high up. If Caroline isn't immune, none of us are.

"I went to Jack first," she continues.

Jack shrinks a little at the mention of his name.

"I've known for weeks something was up with you. But

you haven't been self-medicating because you feel guilty about cheating. You feel guilty because you knew this was coming."

We all turn to glare at Jack, who just shrugs. "Yeah, okay? My dad told me the whole thing two weeks ago, right down to popping pills in the champagne. But what was I supposed to do, go on Instagram and blast it to the world? Cause a mass panic? It was already too late."

He walks over to Caroline, shoulders slumped and hands out, like he's begging for mercy. "I'm sorry."

Caroline holds her palm out to stop him. "Don't even, Jack."

"Pari and I saw the model of the Gateway bunkers," I say. "And the map. It's in Texas. Webber will be president, and his buds will all be generals."

"How the hell did you find that out?" Jack stares at me, aghast.

"The Red Room," I say. "The one you gave us directions to."

He snatches a bottle of whiskey and pulls the cork out. "This is why they needed to keep me informed. And let me in the fucking Red Room!"

"Shut up!" Pari, Max, Caroline, and I all say together.

I have an idea. Maybe I can use his frustration to get some information out of him. "Do you at least know how everyone is supposed to get from here to some desert bunker in Texas?"

He takes a swig of the whiskey. "Helicopters. Big-ass military helicopters that Webber bought and Gregory rigged so they'd be shielded from the flare. There are twelve of those bad boys on their way here to pick us up right now."

My fists clench at my sides, and rage burns through me

like a wildfire. "We have to stop this. It's bad enough that he's known this solar flare was coming for god knows how long and didn't warn people, but now he's going to kidnap people and force them into his cult. I'm not going to be one of his followers. I refuse. Who's with me?"

Caroline puts her hands on her hips. "No fucking way I'm letting him *Handmaid's Tale* me."

"Please," Max says. "We're way past the red cloaks here." She turns to me. "I'm in, obviously. The way I see it, we either fight or die."

Pari nods and taps her cane on the floor like a judge's gavel. "We fight."

"Burn this place to the ground if we have to," I say.

Jack is unsurprisingly quiet. We all turn to him expectantly.

"Jack?" Caroline says. "This is your chance to redeem yourself a little bit. Are you with us, or are you against us?"

He scrubs a hand down his face. "I'm with you, Caroline. Always."

My gut tells me he's lying. "You'd turn on your dad? On the 'family'? What's in it for you?"

He shrugs. "Besides Caroline? A clear conscience. Obviously I couldn't stop the solar flare. But it's not too late to stop Webber. We can still tell everyone what he's doing, we can still save them from being lured to the Gateway."

I cross my arms over my chest. "I tried that already, remember?"

Jack gives me a look. "But this time, they'll be more suggestible. That's the whole point of the drugs. If we can get to them before Webber, and we can find another way out of the factory, then we can help everyone escape before the helicopters even get here."

The group exchanges suspicious glances. That's a tall order.

"Listen," Jack continues. "Webber always has a contingency plan. There's no way he would lock this building down without a way to undo it. A secret button or fail-safe, in case something went wrong. We just need to find it."

I can't help but wonder if this is all pointless. The dean has clearly spent years building relationships with Webber Academy members, so much that they all believe they're his family, just like my parents did. Just like I did. Even after we reveal the truth to them, how many of them would still follow him over the edge of the cliff? They could hear what we have to say and then still choose to join Webber in his new world.

But at least they would have a choice. Even if we save one person from his clutches, that's something. The people deserve a choice.

The silence is thick with hesitation, and Jack takes a step toward all of us. "Come on, guys. We don't have much time. Let me help you."

"Fine," Caroline says. "But one wrong move, and I'll make sure you regret it."

Jack gives her a small smile. "Everyone will still be in the ballroom. Webber and his circle should be celebrating in the Red Room by now, waiting until the drugs kick in for everyone else."

"Back to the ballroom, then," Caroline says, and she pulls

open the oil-painting door again. I start to sweat just thinking about getting back in there.

"Wait," Jack says. "I know an easier way to get there from here. One that won't give us blisters."

Caroline shakes her head. "This will be faster."

"Come on," he says. "You're not the only one who knows shortcuts around here. It's just through that door."

"Fine." Caroline shuts the galley door and we let Jack take the lead.

The halls he takes us down look familiar to me, but then again, I've spent so much time racing around this factory tonight that I've probably made laps. He shows us to a set of double doors and pushes them open.

It's the gentleman's lounge, with the giant stuffed bear and pool tables. My gut screams at me to run the other way. "He's leading us in the wrong direction."

The girls stop, and Jack groans, like he's exhausted by me. "Are you giving me a chance or not?"

This is not the way to the ballroom. I know it isn't. I stand firm. "Not."

Jack turns to Caroline. "You trust me, don't you?"

She takes a step back from him, shaking her head. "Not more than I trust Waverly."

That must really piss him off, because he grabs Caroline by the hair at the back of her neck and pulls her into the lounge with him. He throws her over his shoulder like a prize and starts running. She punches him in the back and we chase after him, yelling at him to put her down.

He sprints into the smaller cigar room, the one Jeff Ramsey was murdered in, and kicks the door closed behind him. Max makes it there first, pummeling her fists on the door, and with Pari and me right behind her we manage to shove it open. Jack tries to force us out, but it's three against one—four against one, once Caroline, whom he'd dumped on the couch, gets her feet under her—and eventually we push our way in, almost tumbling over one another.

The bloodstained carpet sits damp and dark in the center. I spin around just in time to see Jack push the door closed and lock it behind him. Then he removes his mask and throws it onto the floor. He pulls one of those damn walkie-talkies out of his jacket pocket. "I've got them," he says into it while he watches us from under hooded eyes. "Cigar room. Hurry."

I glare at him, fuming. He just smiles.

"Old school," he explains, pointing to the walkie-talkie. "Battery powered and secured with tech to protect from the flare. Gregory designed them especially for tonight. Before his terrible accident, of course."

Caroline runs at him. "You son of a bitch!"

He swallows the key to the door before she can snatch it from him. I ram into him, knocking him to the floor. Max, Pari, and I hold him down while Caroline whales on him, hitting him again and again.

"If you think we won't cut you open to get that key," I snarl, "you've got another think coming."

Pari gets up, goes to the door, and leans one hand on her cane while the other grips the doorknob and tries to shake it open. "Shit. Shitshitshit." She turns to me. "Give me two of your bobby pins."

I pull two of the dozens of bobby pins out of my hair, causing thick strands to fall loose around my shoulders. Pari slips them into the keyhole, muttering curse words as she tries to crack the lock. Her cane rests on her hip.

Jack pushes Caroline and Max off of him, then jumps to his feet. He takes a sword from one of the suits of armor by the fireplace and points it at them, warning them to stay away. Begrudgingly, they do.

Then, with the cocky air of someone who has succeeded in his evil plan, Jack sits on an armchair against a wall, resting the sword over his lap. "There's no use fighting it."

I glare at him as he straightens his suit and bow tie. Without his mask, the dead look in his eyes is clearer than ever before. Polished swords and silver knives hang on the wall above his head, sharp edges pointed toward him like arrows warning us of his intentions.

He doesn't need to say anything else. He has chosen which side he's on. When it comes to choosing between his father and the rest of us, his father will always win. Spoiled rich boys don't give up their power easily, and Jack is spoiled to the core.

"You were never with us," I say, glaring at him. "Not even for a second."

"What did you expect?" Jack asks. "You really think I'd go against Owen, against the family, my own flesh and blood? For what? To help you and the Scooby Squad escape into the darkness? You have no idea what's going down outside. At least with the family, we know where we stand. Owen wants to build a world where everyone is the same. None of the identity politics, none of the infighting, none of the distractions. We will finally be free. And more important, we'll be protected."

"Yeah," Pari scoffs. "Like prisoners are protected in a cell." She gives up on trying to unlock the door, throwing the pins to the floor with a frustrated huff.

I nod. "I'd rather take my chances out in the real world than bow down to whatever fucked-up society Webber wants to build."

"Lucky for you," he says, "you aren't invited."

No surprise there. People like me aren't included in Webber's vision for a utopian society. Whatever this new world is going to be, it won't be welcoming to people like me. It won't be friendly to people like my mom. I can't imagine it will be safe for Black and brown folks like Max and Pari, either.

"How could you do this to us?" Caroline asks Jack, her voice cracking with emotion. "How could you do this to *me*?"

Jack gives her a sympathetic look. "I did this *for* you, baby. We'll be happy in the new world. In the Gateway, we'll be safe. We'll have everything we've ever wanted."

"I won't have my dad," she says.

Jack shakes his head. "I'm so sorry about that. I really am. But he lost sight of the vision. He turned against the family. But you still have me. Your dad had a condo ready in the bunker for the both of you, it's still yours. We'll get married and start a family and prepare for our return to the city once everything has calmed down."

"Married?" Caroline recoils. "None of that is going to happen, Jack, because I'm not going with you."

He glares at her. "You have to. Gregory secured the bunker with fingerprint technology. To unlock it, we need the thumbprints of Owen and all the generals. But in case something happened to them, there's a backup: next-of-kin thumbprints. And now we need the next of kin to open General Sinclair's bunker, and that's you, baby. You're one of the keys."

Caroline's mouth falls open.

"Do you get it now?" Jack asks.

That's why everyone has been acting like Caroline is some kind of savior. With Gregory out of the picture, they need her thumbprint to open a bunker and complete the Gateway. Without her, it doesn't work.

"Just wait until you see the place, Caroline," he says dreamily. "It's going to be amazing."

I scoff. "Yeah. For you. We're not letting you take Caroline anywhere."

He turns to me, his face contorting into anger. "Shut the fuck up, bitch. I'm so sick of your shit. You shouldn't even be here."

Something possesses me then. I don't know if it's hurt or anger or courage or a mix of all three, but whatever it is makes me storm over to the second suit of armor beside the fireplace. I wrap my fingers around the cool, engraved handle of the sword and pull it out of the knight's clasped hands. It's not as heavy as I expected, and I move it through the air easily.

Jack doesn't expect any of this from me, so it takes him a second to react. He stands up to defend himself, but in his haste, he drops his sword to the floor. I hold mine out in front of me, the sharp point aimed directly at him.

"Whoa, whoa," he says as he waves his hands up, playing innocent. He steps away until his back is against the wall, and the edge of my sword is kissing the bare skin of his neck.

"What did you say to me?" I ask, my teeth bared, like a lion about to feast on her prey.

"Nothing," he squeaks. "I didn't say anything."

I tilt my head to the side. "All you do is lie. Just like your father lies about hiking up those drug prices."

Recognition flashes in Jack's eyes. "That's what this is about?" I dig the sword a little deeper into his neck.

Jack lifts his head up higher, trying to lean away from the blade. "Look, those drugs? They upped the price tag so that they'd sell less product."

Max makes a face beside me. "That makes no sense."

Jack sighs. "Listen. The fewer boxes of those pills they sold, the more they'd be able to move to the bunker. And by charging more, they'd make up the difference, you know? They could make the same amount of money without losing more inventory. What I'm saying is, those drugs are at the bunker. Enough for years and years. We're going to have all the medication we need. Don't you see? Webber really has thought of everything."

I grit my teeth and twist the sword. "Except my mom was conveniently left off the invite list to that precious bunker. He didn't think of her. Your dad didn't think of her. So don't give me that bullshit story that they were doing it out of the goodness of their hearts."

Blood runs down his neck. I watch the droplet as it leaves a red streak on his skin.

"Waverly," Pari says from behind me. "Don't."

I don't take my eyes off of Jack. "Why? Why shouldn't I?"

Caroline steps beside me and places a hand on my shoulder. "Don't let him do this to you." She slowly reaches her other hand out and places it on top of mine. I don't realize my hands are trembling until she touches me. I feel frozen in place, air trapped in my lungs, head buzzing with adrenaline. Caroline gently pushes my hands down, forcing me to lower the sword from Jack's neck. The moment the blade hangs by my side, Jack jumps away from me, swearing up a storm.

"You're crazy," he says. He wipes at his neck, flinching when he touches the tiny little cut there. "Fucking crazy bitch."

I take a step forward, but Caroline and Pari hold me back.

"He's not worth it," Pari says to me. "We need to focus on getting out of here before security shows up."

And that's when I remember. "There's a secret door. Behind one of these bookshelves."

I turn my back on Jack, but he isn't giving up on the fight. I hear the slice of a blade against the floor, and before I can react, I feel an intensely sharp pain in my right shoulder. I let out a scream and fall onto my hands and knees. I clench my jaw to stop my cries from spilling out. He fucking stabbed me.

"Get back!" Jack yells at the others.

Pain radiates down my arm, but my anger burns even more. I stand back up and turn around to face him, and then I swing my sword high. He isn't expecting me to fight back, I can tell by the look of complete shock on his face. My sword connects with his and the sound of our blades sparking together fills the air.

I have no idea what I'm doing, but neither does he. The difference is that I have a lifetime's worth of rage spurring me on, and he's never had anyone stand up to him before in his life until tonight.

The sword vibrates in my hands as it clashes with his, making the pain in my shoulder deepen. I can't give up now, but I don't know how much longer I can hold the sword. It must only weigh about three pounds, but the way it is pulling on my hurt arm is killing me. Jack tries to swipe me again, the sharp edge narrowly missing my ribs this time.

My instinct is to jump back, retreat, but I push ahead. I let out a loud groan as I swing my sword down violently. It slices right into Jack's right hand, leaving a clean, deep cut starting at the base of his thumb and ending at his wrist. Blood pours out instantly, and he cries out in pain as the sword drops from his grip.

He glares at me as he clutches at his wrist. "You're going to pay for this."

Footsteps rumble outside the door. Jack's backup is on

their way. Sweat prickles down my back. We need to get out of here.

I throw the sword down and rush over to the back wall, pressing and pulling on books and knocking over trinkets, trying to find a lever or button or whatever triggers this damn door to open. Dusty old books fall to the floor around me, and that's when I see it. A miniature knight built into the shelving.

Keys jangle on the other side of the door. I reach up and pull on the knight's sword, and it flips down. The bookcase swings open with a long, slow creak.

"Quick!" I wave the girls over. Jack jumps up, holding the sword out again, trying to block their path. With my good arm, I pick up one of the bronze globes of the Earth from the shelf and slam it over his head. He stumbles sideways onto the couch, clutching his temple.

Max, Pari, and Caroline rush past him and through the door, and then I follow. We push the bookcase closed just as the other door starts to swing open.

And then we flee like bats out of hell.

CHAPTER NINETEEN

Y ou're not gonna like where this leads," I tell them as we hobble down the dark, medieval stairwell. My skin crawls at the memory of what awaits us, but it's our only way out. Mason has probably already sent his guards to hunt us down.

"Waverly," Pari calls up to me. "Can you . . ." She doesn't need to finish her question. I know these dark, spiral dungeon stairs are not accessibility-friendly.

"I'm coming!" I hurry down to her and give her my arm. We walk down each uneven step together, her cane slipping every now and then. But we make it.

I push the door open and step back into the cursed, abandoned storeroom. The flashlight I dropped on my escape earlier sits in the threshold, light fading and dim. In my panic, not only did I lose it, but I didn't switch it off. Perfect.

I pick it up and start leading the girls through the basement of horrors.

"Waverly," Pari says, her voice low. "What. The. Actual. Fuck."

I shrug, wincing from the cut on my shoulder. "It was either take our chances in here or stay in the cigar room and be captured by the goon squad."

Pari shakes her head. "That's not what I meant. You're bleeding."

"Oh." I twist my neck around to try to look at my wound, but it's too dark to see it properly. "Is it bad?"

Pari takes the flashlight from me and shines it on my shoulder. "Listen, it's not pretty, but it's not, like, gonna kill you. We should patch it up though."

"Yeah," I say sarcastically. "Just let me fetch my first aid kit."

Pari narrows her eyes at me. "If you weren't already injured, I'd slap you for being snarky."

Max and Caroline move one of the dusty old sewing tables in front of the door to block Mason and his team from following us. Then Caroline points at it and nods at me.

"Sit," she says. "I might be able to patch it up."

"How?" I ask.

"Just. Sit." Caroline slips her silky, elbow-length gloves off.

We don't have time for this, but we also don't have time to argue, so I do as she asks and jump backward into a seated position on the table like I'm in a doctor's office.

"Max, take this." Caroline pulls off one of her long gloves and hands it to her, then the other. "Pari, shine the light on the cut." Then, in a surprising turn of events, Caroline reaches her hand into the bodice of her dress, then pulls out the padding of the built-in bra and grins at me. "Don't you ever wonder why my boobs always look so good?" She makes a face as she reaches deeper into her dress and peels body tape off of her skin. Her cleavage falls slightly, and I can't help but giggle.

"Tie the gloves together," she says to Max while she gently places the bra pads against my wound and uses the tape to secure them tight.

I flinch a little at the pressure, the pain searing from the middle of my back to my shoulder blade like a line of fire. I squeeze my eyes shut and grind my teeth together. Not gonna lie, it hurts like hell. Fuck Jack. I hate that he got one over on me like that.

"I swear to god," I say through gritted teeth. "If I see Jack again . . ."

"You and me both," Caroline says, finishing my thought for me. "Now, hold still. This is going to sting."

I don't tell her that "sting" was a major understatement. She wraps her long evening gloves around my opposite shoulder, diagonally across my body, so they keep the padding in place over my cut, then ties them into a tight knot just near my ribs.

"There," she says once it's done. "It kind of looks like a sash."

"A bloody sash," Pari says, making me laugh. "How does it feel?"

"Fine," I lie. "Who knew boob tape could patch up a sword wound? Secrets of femmes!"

Caroline laughs and pushes her breasts up proudly. "You're welcome."

"Into the nightmare we go," Pari says as she looks out over the mannequins before us.

"It's fine," Max says, totally keeping her cool. "They're just dummies." She taps one on the nose, and its head falls clean off. We all scream.

In all the panic, I trip backward and land in a pile of dis-membered arms and legs. Pari screams again, and the flashlight falls from her grip, spinning like a top on the concrete. I rest my hands behind me, trying to climb out of the mountain of plastic and rubber, but my shoulder isn't as strong as it usually is. I struggle to get up, then realize one of the arms feels soft, almost warm.

"What is this?"

Just as I ask that question, the flashlight stops spinning, the light landing on a face that looks very different from all the others. It's bloodied, the eyes lopsided, the mouth hanging open. I recognize him instantly.

"Jeff Ramsey," I say, almost breathlessly. This is where Ma-son dragged his body to, thinking no one would ever find him. Pari screams my name and pulls me up frantically while Max and Caroline let out chilling cries at the sight of Jeff's dead body.

My hands tremble as I lean down to pick up the flashlight. Then I close my eyes and take a few seconds to gather my wits. I don't know how much more of this night I can take.

"Okay, it's okay," I say, more to myself than the others. "Just breathe. Breathe, and start walking."

Caroline pulls her mask off, hunches over, and throws up all over the old sewing table. Max rubs her back with one hand while covering her own mouth with the other.

"I'm okay," Caroline says. "We need to keep going."

I grab Pari's hand, and she takes Max's, and Max takes Caroline's. Then we start rushing through the narrow path in the middle of the room, the same one I pushed my way through just a couple of hours ago. God, I hope the freight elevator on the other end is going to work this time.

Creepy little scratching sounds rush around us as we go. "Whatever you do," I whisper, "don't look down."

I hear Caroline whimper at the end of the line. "I'm not even going to ask why."

"Good idea," I reply.

When we get to the other side, I shine the weakening light onto the button for the elevator. Oh, right. The button fell off last time I tried this. Trying my luck, because what else do I have at this point, I pick the round button tab up off the floor, and pop it back in its hole. I let my finger hover over it for a second, suck in a deep breath, and press it.

Nothing.

"Fuck."

"What?" Caroline asks.

I press the button repeatedly: *taptaptaptaptap*.

It falls to the floor again. Can't say I'm surprised. But I am officially out of ideas.

"Oh," Caroline says. "Fuck."

"Move," Max says.

I step aside and watch as she bends down to inspect the button hole. "There's probably a wire loose. Hold the flashlight steady. And give me one of those bobby pins."

I do as she asks, pulling another pin from my hair, and she uses her teeth to bend it until it's straight. Then she slips it under a loose piece of paneling around the hole and uses her other hand to rip it right off the wall. She holds a hand out. "Flashlight, please."

I oblige, and she gets to work like a surgeon on the mess of wires, using her long nails to separate them.

Heavy footsteps rumble from the stairwell on the other side of the room.

"They're coming," Caroline says.

Max holds a finger up to silence her. After a tense moment, something clicks, and the freight elevator roars to life somewhere above us.

"Yes, Max!" we all cheer, and high-five her.

"I'm going to MIT for robotics," she says proudly, but then her smile fades. "At least, I *was*."

My excitement mutates into sadness, the reminder of how uncertain all our futures are now casting a darkness over me that rivals any blackout. The elevator arrives, and we all cram quickly inside. Caroline is about to press the button for the ballroom level when the elevator shoots up. The force of its trajectory knocks us off our feet, and we hit the floor. The walls screech, and we scream, and gravity weighs me down so hard I can't even lift my hands up to cover my ears.

A few terrifying moments later, the elevator stops.

"Ow," Pari says.

"What the hell was that?" Max asks.

"Oh, shit," Caroline groans. "Are we stuck in this thing?"

Max gets up and tries to pry open the door. "No. Nope. We're getting out. We're not stuck."

But five minutes pass, then ten, and we're still sitting in the shoddy elevator, only now it's getting so hot we're all sweating. The air is getting thicker, and the silence is getting louder. I hate this. It's giving me too much time to think. And the more I think, the more I sit here and replay everything I've seen tonight, or imagine everything that could be happening outside these walls right now, the more panicked I'll become. Sometimes, the quiet of my mind is the worst place to be. I'm safer out here, where I'm being chased down by killers and kings, not up inside my own head, because at least out here, I have friends.

"I'm trying the doors again," Max says. Caroline gets up to help her this time.

Pari reaches out and takes my hand, squeezing it. "My dad is supposed to be on a plane right now," she whispers, her voice so quiet I can barely hear her. "Do you think he's okay?"

"I think so," I say, trying to sound hopeful even though I'm worried for her. "If old-school radio communications are still working, then that must mean the air traffic control towers are still able to guide planes into landing, right?" I have no idea what I'm talking about, but all we have left right now is hope.

Pari lifts her mask up to wipe stray tears from her eyes, and I pull her into a hug. "Hey," I say into her soft hair. "We don't even know for sure that London has been hit as bad as we have. He's probably more worried about you right now."

She nods against my shoulder. "I know. I just hope that I didn't use my last conversation with him to blow him off."

I think back to when he dropped us off at my house, how annoyed I was at him, and guilt ties a knot in my stomach.

Then I think of my parents. I try to remember the last conversation I had with them, but I come up blank. We drove to school together this morning—god, was that only this morning? But we didn't talk. Not really. Dad listened to his music, Mom spent the ride trying to hide her pain, and I sat in the back seat staring out the window and making myself anxious about another school day.

What if that was the last time I'll ever see them? They don't know where I am. They can't get in contact with me. They might not have heard the president's address, might not know why the sky is lit up like the Fourth of July or why the power is out. They could be out looking for me. They could be stuck in traffic on the Queensboro Bridge. They could have gotten into an accident or be trapped on the subway.

If I even make it out of here without getting kidnapped or killed, how the hell am I supposed to get home? The trains won't be working. If by some miracle buses and taxis can still drive, I seriously doubt they'd be operating as usual. If car engines still have some life in them, maybe, *maybe,* there'll still be some taxi drivers around, but I can never afford a ride in a normal circumstance, and who knows how much a trip from Lower Manhattan out to Queens would cost during a literal apocalypse scenario. I could walk, but it would take hours. I wouldn't make it home until well after the sun is up.

I suck in a deep, shaky breath. The last thing I need right now is a panic attack. But even just the fear of an impending attack makes my heart pound even harder in my chest. My fingers start to tingle with pins and needles.

I lean back, breaking my hug with Pari, feeling claustrophobic and overheated. My chest rises and falls rapidly, and suddenly I'm struggling to breathe. I feel like I'm being crushed by an invisible weight. I take my mask off and try to suck some air into my lungs.

"Whoa," Pari says holding her hands out for me. "Waverly, are you okay? You're even paler than usual."

I pull my legs to my chest, rocking back and forth. The emotions swirling inside me threaten to spill out, and I'm worried if I let myself cry or scream or focus too long on everything that's happened, I'll lose control. I've already lost control of too much tonight. I just want to go home, but I'm scared of what I'll find the minute I go back out into the city. I start pulling out the leftover bobby pins holding my hair in place. I can't stand them digging into my scalp for a second longer.

The elevator doors open, snapping me out of my panic. I scramble out and catch my breath. It takes me a few moments to collect myself, and I know I'm still barely holding myself together, but at least I'm out of the elevator. As long as I can keep moving, I'll be okay.

That's when I realize where we are. "The Red Room."

We're on a different part of the penthouse floor than Pari and I visited earlier, but this is definitely the same place. And this time it's filled with people. The four of us freeze, as if standing still will make us invisible. But to my relief and surprise, no one seems to notice our arrival. They're too busy celebrating.

There've got to be almost fifty people mingling around, with most spilling out onto a balcony to watch the show unfolding in the sky above. All their masks are gone, their bow ties undone and heels kicked off. Everyone is completely wasted. Words slurring, hair mussed up, unable-to-control-the-volume-levels-of-their-voices wasted—which will definitely work in our favor. I name-check some of them as politicians from both sides of the aisle. Then there are media moguls, some faculty, even a few big-name celebrities who somehow got in on the deal. It's impossible to tell if they're so drunk because they've been partying too hard or because they unknowingly drank the drugged champagne and are starting to feel the effects. Either way, the Red Room is a mess of cackling laughter and stumbling grown-ass adults. No one will recognize us if they can't even see straight.

A gold bucket of oysters and ice sits on a dining table, along with plates of shrimp, lobster, and caviar. The bar is stocked with wine, champagne, scotch, rum . . . all the most expensive bottles money can buy. Clearly, the dean has saved the most extravagant delicacies for his nearest and dearest co-conspirators.

Tall candelabras are lined up along the walls, casting moving shadows over the portraits hanging in gold frames behind them. Oil paintings of the Webber lineage, including one of Ash as a child with both her parents.

Unlike the ones in the rest of the factory, the arched

windows in rows on either side of the room aren't shuttered. Outside, the expanse of stars seems to have grown, the clouds burning electric blue from a light source somewhere above them, sharp streaks spreading like roots. It's like lightning has been trapped in the ether, searching for a way to Earth.

Across the East River, billowing smoke rises from all over Brooklyn. I hope it's been caused by overloaded wires and it's not a sign that chaos has already erupted. New York has faced disaster before, and every time we have come together. I have to hold on to hope that we'll do the same again. Webber and his cronies plan to abandon this place, but I will always choose New York. It's my home.

Just as I'm wondering where the dean is, I hear his uproarious laughter from the balcony. I peek through the glass and see him, elbow resting on the ledge, surrounded by worshippers, crystal glasses touching their greedy mouths as the city burns around them.

The world isn't ending with a bang or a whimper, but with the pop of champagne.

I can't believe I ever aspired to fit in with these people. It's shameful that it took an explosion of protons and electrons from the sun to finally wake me up, but now that my eyes are wide open, I can't ever go back.

Just then, I spot Ash coming inside from the balcony. She walks over to the portrait of her as a child with her parents, staring up at it. Just the sight of her draws me in like a magnet. Maybe I'm making a mistake, maybe I'm a pathetic, naive, lovesick girl. Or maybe I'm just tired of running around this damned factory searching for clues when the person with all the answers is right in front of me. Quietly, I sneak away from the others to talk to her.

Before I can even say anything, Ash shakes her head. "You never give up, do you?"

"I'm just trying to get out of here," I say.

She sighs. "You can't win against him, Waverly. I've tried." Ash turns to me, and her eyes widen at the sight of my bloodied arm. "What happened? Are you okay?"

"Do you actually care?" The words come out bitter on my tongue, and she winces.

"I deserved that," she says. "But I do care. You're all I care about, Waverly. Don't you see that I'm trying to protect you?"

I want to believe her, but actions speak louder than words. I decide to ask the question that's been lingering on my mind all night, and my mouth goes dry. "How long have you known?"

A tear falls onto her cheek. "Since that weekend. Fourth of July."

Since the last time we were together. My heart drops into my stomach. That's the answer I was afraid of. The answer that turns her into one of them, that makes me question if I can really trust her or not. I want so badly to trust her.

"That day," she says, avoiding my gaze, "after you left, he came home. That was the day he told me everything. He told me that he wasn't in Texas for a political fundraiser, he was there to oversee the final construction days of a bunker that will help us survive an earth-shattering event. He wouldn't tell me what or where or how, just that it was only a matter of time before the world as we knew it changed forever, and it was our responsibility to shepherd people into a new way of living."

She wipes another tear off her cheek. "He told me he'd been monitoring everything. My phone, email, social media. He had access to all of it. And Mason, he'd been following me, us, everywhere we went. Nothing was private. I was disgusted. I was terrified. And then he sent me away. He made me keep up appearances. I had to take photos and selfies and he would approve them and post them to my Instagram. But he controls everything, Waverly. I can't escape. But you still can."

If this is all true, she's been a prisoner of her father this whole time, and if we don't unlock this building, everyone here will face the same fate.

"We're going to help people escape," I say firmly. "You can help us."

She gives me a look, and I can't tell if it's sympathy or admiration or both.

"If you stay," she says quietly, "he'll take you, too."

CHAPTER TWENTY

There was no way you could have told people?" I ask Ash. "Told me? I would have helped you."

"He was watching everything I did, Waverly," she snaps, and I feel bad for questioning her. "Besides, even if I could have told you, would you have believed me?"

"Of course I would have."

Her eyebrows rise, and she opens her mouth to say something but then closes it again. She looks genuinely surprised at my response, but I'm telling the truth. If she had told me all this, I would have been scared and shocked, but I would have listened to what she had to say. I would have believed her. It hurts to know she thought I would have done anything else.

"Well," she says, finally. "I didn't think anyone would listen. Who am I? I mean, can you imagine world leaders listening to an eighteen-year-old girl who says the world is ending, but she doesn't know when, or how? They'd have me committed, and to be honest, I don't think my father would have stopped them." She glances toward the balcony, where Webber continues to laugh like he has the world in the palms of his hands. "He will do literally anything to protect his precious Gateway."

"You drank the champagne," I say, suddenly remembering. "I saw the guards drugging the drinks."

She shakes her head. "He wouldn't do that to me. He needs me too much right now. He keeps calling me his right-hand man. I'm supposed to help him lead everyone to the bunker."

"You don't have to do this." I take her hands in mine and squeeze them. "You don't have to follow him anymore. You can be your own person, make your own decisions."

A frown forms on her beautiful face. "I'm afraid."

"We all are," I say. "Hell, I'm terrified. But if you follow him, the hold he has on you will get tighter and tighter. You'll *never* be free."

"I can trust you?" she asks me. Her voice shakes.

I nod. "Of course you can. Not just me, but all of us." I gesture to the girls waiting by the elevator. "You're not in this alone anymore, Ash."

Her bottom lip trembles. "I missed you so much. I thought of you every day."

More laughter booms from outside, and she cowers. I pull her into a shadowy corner, out of view from everyone else. She takes my mask off, and it feels so good to be seen by her. I reach up and wipe her tears with the back of my hand, and then she leans in and kisses me.

At first, it's hard and urgent, then soft and tender. I try to

let the feel of her lips burn in my mind, take in every movement, the way her breath catches, how her hands reach up to
trace my jaw. I wish I could tattoo this feeling onto my skin.

Then, like she's suddenly remembering where we are, she
pulls away. "If we're going to get people out of here, we need
to be quick." She helps me put my mask on, then keeps talking.
"There's a code. No one knows about it but me and my dad. It
unlocks the factory."

I gasp. "Are you serious?"

"The keypad is in a surveillance room one floor down."

I take her hand and lead her over to the others, and give
them a quick explainer as we head down the stairs.

"Yes, Ash!" Pari says, patting her on the back. "You're doing the right thing." Ash nods, but I can tell she's still terrified.

We follow her onto the floor below as she opens a door
into a dark room filled with a handful of guards sitting
around.

"What are you doing?" she asks them. The guards look at
each other, like they're confused. Ash sighs. "My dad has been
trying to call you on those walkie-talkie things. He needs you
in the basement. Dissenters are hiding in the maze."

They rush out of the room, and we step inside. Most of the
screens aren't even working, and the ones that are glitch repeatedly, fading in and out of static. They've no doubt been affected by the flare, but I recognize the ballroom on the screens
that do work. Four cameras show different angles of the dance
floor and mezzanine.

Ash steps over to the keypad on the wall. Something about

how easily those henchmen believed her, how they immediately did what she told them to do, makes me uneasy. She really does have a lot of power. How do I know she's actually willing to give that up, for me?

Her fingers tap the keypad and she hits Enter. It flashes red. "Huh?"

Caroline takes a step closer to Ash, watching over her shoulder. Ash's fingers shake as she enters numbers again. Another flash of red in response.

"Ash?" I ask. "Are you sure—"

"I know it!" she snaps. "You can trust me." She reaches a hand out to the keypad again, but Caroline stops her.

"I don't know if we can." Caroline steps in between Ash and the keypad. "What happens if you enter the code incorrectly too many times, Ash?"

"I know the code," Ash says. "Get out of my way."

They're standing so close, just like they were at the beginning of the night, when I saw them arguing in the corner of the mezzanine.

"What were you two fighting about?" I ask. "Earlier tonight, I mean. I saw you."

Ash turns slightly, but doesn't meet my eyes. All I want is to reach out and touch her, to feel her touch me back, to have some reassurance.

Caroline glares at her. "I was trying to get her to help me. To tell me what her father's plans are. But she said I was being paranoid."

Everything Ash has told me tonight falls into question. What if it's all been lie after lie?

"I'm sorry," Ash says. "You don't understand, he's watching me all the time. Telling you the truth would have put you in danger."

"We're already in danger," Max says.

Ash sighs. "I know the code, okay? It's my birthday. I get that you don't trust me, but let me prove it to you. Let me enter the code and unlock the building, then you'll know you can trust me." She locks eyes with me, and I want more than anything to believe her.

"Let her do it," I say.

Pari nudges me. "You sure?"

"If it doesn't work, then we find another way." God, I hope I can trust her.

Caroline begrudgingly steps aside, and Ash lifts her fingers to the keypad. I step closer this time, watching intently as she presses each button. But on the last two digits, the year she was born, she hesitates. And then she enters another date instead.

"Ash!" is all I can say before alarms sound. Ash stands there, staring at the numbers, seemingly unbothered by the ear-piercing bells she just set off.

On the screens, guards jump into action. The dean and his friends stop partying on the Red Room balcony and disappear from view.

They're all coming for us.

Pari takes me by the hand, trying to pull me out of the room to run. I can't take my eyes off of Ash. The girl I thought I knew. The girl I loved even after she abandoned me, and whom I have to try to stop loving now that she's betrayed me worse than she ever has—worse than I ever thought she could.

I run through the halls, trying to process what just happened. This feels like another thing that doesn't make sense, a puzzle piece that doesn't match with the picture.

With Dean Webber, there were red flags. Pari practically tugged on his red flags and waved them in front of me, but I ignored them because it was easier. Safer. That was the biggest mistake I've ever made in my life, and now I'm paying for it.

But with Ash? There were no red flags until she disappeared.

At least, I didn't think there were. Her abandoning me on her birthday was a red flag that I forgave her for. I just kept forgiving.

And now I'm doubting everything. I'm questioning everything I've ever seen, heard, believed before today. It feels like I woke up and discovered everything I'd thought was real was just an unstable fantasy, something I took for granted but couldn't actually rely on, right down to the light switch in my bedroom.

Caroline opens a door into a stairwell and we hide in there, catching our breath.

"I'm sorry," I say. "I thought we could trust her. I thought I knew her."

Caroline laughs dryly. "Funny considering I've never even seen you talk to her before tonight."

"They were just making out in that Red Room, Caroline," Max explains. She looks at me. "I saw you sneak off and I followed. I'm sorry, but I don't trust anyone right now."

Caroline's jaw drops, and I brace myself for whatever might come next.

"Wait," Caroline says, waving her hands around as she tries to catch up. "You and Ash? Like, together?"

I can't tell from her tone if she's mad or not, so I don't say anything. She knows I'm queer, so she can't be pissed about that. Maybe she's annoyed that I kept such a big secret from her? Ugh. People are confusing and my brain is too fried to figure this out right now. Pari stands by my side, and I can tell by the way she's watching Caroline that she's ready to fight for me if she has to. But god, I hope she doesn't have to. With all the fighting we've been doing tonight, I don't want to defend who I love, too.

Caroline's brow furrows; then a small smile breaks out on her face. "So you were the one she was sneaking around with last year?" She tips her head back, letting out a laugh. "Man, I was way off. I thought it was Lance."

My shoulders relax a little, and I let out a breath I didn't know I was holding. Ash and I kept our relationship secret out of fear, and now I'm wondering if the main person she was afraid of was her dad. Or maybe I just didn't matter enough to her, maybe she didn't want to be seen with me in public, maybe I was all part of her game.

Tears start to well in my eyes, but I fight them back. I don't know if I'll ever be able to forgive Ash for what she's done, but I can't turn my feelings for her off like a light switch. I've spent the last six months trying, and I still love her more today than I ever have.

"She betrayed me," I concede. "She told me she didn't know *what* was going to happen, just that something was coming. Her dad wouldn't even tell her the specifics, that he was monitoring all her texts and socials, having her followed everywhere. But now I don't know what the truth is."

Max shakes her head. "Or maybe you just don't want to admit the truth. People don't just forget their own birthdays."

Caroline leans against the railing of the stairs, looking up and down. "What do we do now?"

CHAPTER TWENTY-ONE

Waverly, calm down," Caroline says. Her voice sounds faraway. I don't know where we are, but it's dark and claustrophobic. I'm rocking back and forth, moving in slow circles. My arms are pressed against my chest, hands clasped, fingers squeezing tight. My gaze is trained on the hem of my dress: watching it drag over the floor in circles helps focus my mind. But I don't need to look up to know that Pari, Caroline, and Max are watching me like I'm a bomb about to detonate.

Max elbows her in the ribs. "Shh! Don't ever tell someone having a meltdown to calm down."

Oh, crap. Max is right. I'm having a meltdown. My brain is fogged like a ship in a storm.

"Waverly," Pari says softly. "What do you need?"

I can't speak. I just hum a noise and shake my head. *Leave me alone, please* is what I want to say. Don't come near me, don't look at me, don't talk to me. Let me soothe myself in peace. But words always fail me when I'm like this. My voice retreats somewhere deep inside me, and I wish I could follow it. I want to hide. I don't want to feel the pain anymore.

"I'm sorry," Max says. "None of this is your fault, Waverly. Ash is the one who screwed us."

"She's right," Caroline says. "We're on your side. We're a team. And we need you."

I nod, I hum more, but I'm not ready to come back yet. I'm so fucking tired. My bones ache from running around this damn factory in heels and a ball gown all night. My blisters have blisters. My stab wound is throbbing so hard it's giving me a headache. But the physical pain doesn't even compare to the heartache I'm feeling.

I've watched two people die tonight. The sound of Frank's head hitting the wall replays in my memory like a stuck vinyl on a record player. My head starts to spin, and I lean against the wall to keep myself standing.

Not only has the world at large changed forever, but my own world has been tipped on its axis. The people I thought that I knew, that I could trust, the community I thought I was part of, the future I've been working so hard to obtain . . . it's all been shattered. I feel broken. The man my parents and I have put all our trust and energy and money into for years has taken his mask off, and underneath he's a monster. The girl I loved just keeps ripping my heart out, and I keep letting her.

I close my eyes while the others try to come up with a plan without me.

"My parents," Max says. "They're still in the ballroom."

I think of my parents, afraid of what they're going through right now. If I could be with them, make sure they're safe, I would. And I will. But until then, I can at least help Max's parents get out of this place.

"The ballroom will still be locked," Caroline says. "And guarded. We could go back down through the dumbwaiter, the way we escaped."

"No," Pari says sternly. "I can't do that again. My muscles are still burning. I just don't have the spoons for another ride on that thing."

"It's okay," Max says. "That would just get us trapped in the ballroom again anyway. We need to find a way to let them out."

"Fire." The word jumps out of my mouth, surprising all of us.

"Um," Pari says. "Waverly? You back?"

"A fire in the building will trigger the emergency release," I say quickly. "Jack mentioned something about it before. The doors will all unlock, and everyone can get out."

I can get out. I can get as far away from this place, from Ash, as possible. And never see her traitorous face again. I switch from rocking back and forth to flapping my wrists. Open my eyes. My body still aches, my heart still hurts, but this idea has given me one more spark of energy.

"We set a fire," Caroline says slowly, as though mulling it over in her head. "The doors open, then we run."

Max takes in a deep breath. "The world is ending, what have we got to lose?"

The kitchen next to the ballroom is empty when we get there. I don't know if the chefs and staff were sent home or if they've been roped into joining the new world, but right now I can't worry about that.

"You three wait in the hall," I say, making it all up as I go. "Once the doors open, you'll need to usher everyone out to safety before the fire spreads."

"And you?" Pari asks.

"I'll be right behind you. It's better if just one of us does this." They leave, looking left and right for guards before entering the hallway.

This is dangerous and risky, but if I've learned anything tonight, it's that I'm capable of more than I ever thought possible.

First things first: I pick up a metal trash can and empty it all over the floor. It stinks, but I'm a New Yorker; I can handle the smell of garbage. Then I look for whatever will burn—paper napkins, parchment, food packaging, even my blood-soaked sash. A stack of empty Cobalt Pharmaceuticals packages in a corner are perfect, and I throw them in, too.

Then I pour some vodka from a bottle I find under the chef's station into the trash can, and add a little cooking oil for good measure. Lastly, I turn the knob on the nearest stove, light a napkin on fire, and throw it into the can.

Flames lick the mouth of the can within seconds. The heat touches my skin, the light bathing me in a fiery glow, and I smile. I smile because now I know I'll do anything to stop the dean from making his twisted dictator dreams come true.

I don't care if I have to burn this whole place down.

I step out of the kitchen with smoke and flames in my wake. The fire alarm blares through every room, and just as I'd hoped, the building unlocks itself.

I outsmarted the high-tech system.

Frank would be proud.

When I walk back into the ballroom, the party rages on like nothing has happened.

The crowd keeps dancing the night away in their couture dresses and expensive tuxedos, drunk and happy. Pari, Caroline, and Max and her parents try to usher small groups of people through the open doors, with no success. It's like they can't even hear the fire alarms. Or maybe the drugs are kicking in and they're starting to fall into a zombielike haze.

Water erupts from the sprinklers above. But still, the party doesn't stop. Some people start cheering, as though this is part of it. I feel like I'm standing on the *Titanic,* screaming at people that we are sinking while they dance even as they drown. Then there are people like Jack and Ash, who would rather tie themselves to the boat than try to swim to safety.

These people have no idea that a powerful sedative is making its way through their systems, slowly phasing out their senses. Soon, their arms and legs will feel heavy, their eyelids will start to droop, their concentration will start to wane. They might get the giggles, like my mom sometimes does when she takes it to help with her pain before bed.

Then Webber and his goons will come and herd them like sheep up to the roof into waiting helicopters. In the morning, they'll wake up groggy, in beds they don't recognize, and discover their lives have been taken from them and replaced with a life of servitude to someone they used to consider family.

Pari makes her way over to me, the tiredness showing in the way she's leaning more on her cane. "It's like they don't want to be saved."

Then they see the smoke coming in from under the kitchen doors, and the switch finally flips.

Parents start pulling their children out of the factory and onto the cobblestoned street. The guards by the entrance chase them, even try to pull them back inside, but survival mode has kicked in. In the choice between fight or flight, the people are choosing flight. Part of me wants to follow them, to run through those doors and into the city. I want to go as far away from here as I can, as far as my feet will take me. I want to run home to my parents and hide. But as I watch Webber's guards flee up the stairs to the mezzanine, running back to their leader, all my rage boils up to the surface.

I turn my back on the open doors. I'm going to stand, and I'm going to fight.

I meet up with Max, Caroline, Pari, and Max's parents, who are shuffling people out of the building.

"If you want to go," I say to them, "I understand. But I'm not done here."

Caroline shakes her head. "You're not the only hero here. There's no way I'm letting Webber get away after what he did to my dad."

"I'm not leaving either," Pari says. "That giant killed Frank. I want revenge."

Max gives her parents a look, and her dad shakes his head. "No, Maxine. You're not going back in there."

Someone in the street calls for help, and Max nods toward the sound. "There are people who need you out here, and people who need me in there."

Her mom takes Max by the hands and grips them tight. "I'm coming with you."

Max and her dad both say "No!" at the same time. "Please," Max continues. Her parents both sigh, like they know what she's about to say. "I know how dangerous it is, but I don't abandon my friends."

Her dad shakes his head again, but this time it means something different. Max hugs him, then pulls her mom into the embrace.

We all exchange determined glances. Whatever happens next, we're in it together.

Max lets go of her parents, who set off to go find others who need help. Then the four of us hitch our dresses up, and we start climbing the stairs.

"That's them!" Mason barks.

We're halfway up the staircase leading to the mezzanine, and he's waiting at the top with his fists clenched by his sides. His guards run down the steps toward us. We turn around to go back down, but guards are racing up to meet us. We're cornered already.

I look around for an escape and notice that one of the chandeliers hanging from the ceiling is within my grasp. I brace myself with one hand on the railing, ignoring the searing stab wound in my shoulder, then reach the other out as far as I can, very aware that losing my balance means a ten-foot drop. My fingers clutch one of the crystal strings hanging down from the thick wood of the chandelier, and I tug it closer. Behind me, a guard gets too close, and Caroline shoves him back. He tumbles down the staircase, rolling head over heels until he lands unconscious on the main level.

I lean out a little farther, gritting my teeth at the pain of my muscles stretching, tightening, pulling against each other. My hand slips, and I fall forward, a scream escaping from me. Suddenly, I feel two hands grasping my waist, lifting me back into a stable position. I glance over my shoulder to see Caroline.

"I got you," she says.

I nod at her and lean out again, taking hold of the chandelier and pulling it over to us.

"Quick!" I say to the others. "Grab on!"

Pari, Max, and I clutch the chandelier. But Caroline hangs back.

"Come on!" I say.

"It's not strong enough to hold us all," Caroline replies. Then she pushes us off the railing, and we hang on to the chandelier for dear life as it swings haphazardly away. I call out to Caroline as she tries to fight off the guards, but there are too many of them.

"Waverly!" Pari says as the chandelier swings over to the opposite staircase. "Catch the railing!"

I lean out and reach for the railing but miss at the last second. "Fuck!"

We start to spin as the chandelier flies back to the first staircase. Guards reach out, trying to grab hold of us, but we kick them away. Caroline screams as she is dragged by her arms up the steps, where Mason waits for her with a smug grin. Jack appears behind him, grinning, too.

On the second swing of the chandelier, I reach out again, my injured arm straining with the effort. And I miss again.

But somehow, we stop.

"Go," Pari grunts. She's stretched out over the chandelier, using the curved handle of her cane to hang on to the railing.

Sweat runs down her forehead as she struggles to hold it in place long enough for Max and me to climb off. Guards race across the dance floor, headed to the second staircase to reach us before we can run.

"Take my hand!" I call out to Pari.

Max and I reach our arms out for her, and she launches herself forward in a literal leap of faith. The force of her jump causes the chandelier to fall out from under her, and for a terrifying second I think she's going to fall to the floor. But Max and I catch her just in time, and the three of us land in a pile on the steps, breathless. Immediately, we're up and moving as fast as we can up to the mezzanine. Guards reach for their Tasers.

"Forget them!" Mason calls back to his men. "We got Caroline. She's the key! Take her to the roof!"

I can't let them take Caroline. If we don't save her, she'll be trapped with them forever.

CHAPTER TWENTY-TWO

"Do you hear that?" Max whispers. We're in a stairwell, slowly making our way to the rooftop, the most likely place they've taken Caroline. One downside I didn't consider when I lit that kitchen fire was that it would also shut down all the elevators. But at least the alarms and sprinklers have stopped.

"I don't hear anything," I reply.

"This . . ." Pari says between breaths. "Is gonna hurt . . . so much. Tomorrow."

I cringe. "I'm so, so sorry."

She gives me a gentle slap on the arm as I help her up another step. "You kicked ass. Unlocked the building. It was a good idea."

"Maybe we should have escaped, too," I wonder out loud. "He's got Caroline now. We should have been smarter."

Max turns on her heels to face me from a few steps above. "No. I don't care if it isn't smart, it was right. The difference between people like us, and people like Jack and Ash, is that we don't stand by while bad guys do bad things. Caroline knows that. That's why she left her dad in the hospital to come here tonight and fight. And that's why we're climbing these stairs, to fight for her."

Damn. Max is good.

"And," Pari adds, "to take Mason down. For Frank."

Max nods. "Sure. That, too." Then she pauses, looks up, and puts her hands on her hips. "Are you sure you don't hear that?"

I listen again, and this time I do hear something. "The helicopters! They're coming."

Pari nudges me to get moving. "We gotta hurry!"

When we finally make it back into the Red Room, it's completely empty, abandoned. The seafood smorgasbord sits mostly untouched on the dining table. Lipstick-stained wineglasses and empty bottles of scotch sit on every available surface. The party is finally over.

"I don't get why we're back here instead of going straight to the roof from the stairs," Max says.

"Jack said there's roof access from here," I explain. "He could've been lying his ass off, but if he wasn't, it could help us get the jump on Webber. He'd never see us coming."

I step out onto the balcony. In the corner, a steel ladder leads up to the roof. The sound of helicopters fills the air. I grab hold of the ladder and start climbing, trying not to think about the fact that I don't have a plan. I don't know what—or *who*—is waiting up there.

But I'm about to find out.

I peek over the edge of the roof.

From here I can see the other two rooftops. They are packed with the party attendees that we couldn't save. Most of them seem to be sitting down, struggling to stay awake. Others are still standing, heads dipped back as they watch the light show among the stars.

That's when I see them. A fleet of large military-grade helicopters coming into view, headed right for us. The first helicopter comes in to land, the gusts of wind hitting me so hard I have to wrap my arms around the ladder to stop myself from slipping. Once it settles onto the roof, I take another peek.

The Gateway generals start climbing aboard the helicopter, the men helping their wives and children through the wide-open doors. I scan the rooftop for Caroline. Webber is by the front of the small crowd, smiling and shaking hands as people pass him on their way to the chopper. He even kisses a few sleeping babies on their foreheads, like a freaking politician trying to win votes.

Ash is a few feet behind him, standing silently by. Maybe it's the strange glow of the sky casting odd shadows on her, but her skin looks pale, almost a sickly gray color. The winds from the helicopter push against her hair and her dress, and every now and then she wobbles, like she's on a boat out at sea and struggling to keep her balance.

No. No, Waverly. Don't get caught up in Ash again. She's chosen her side. Focus on Caroline.

I find her standing close to the wall with a guard holding her tight. Another guard is next to her, hand on his hip holster, like he's just itching for a reason to pull out his Taser. And in front of them are the Bradleys, her kidnappers.

Mrs. Bradley stands proudly next to her husband. She doesn't seem tipsy or drowsy like a lot of the other wives, which means she's been in on this plan the whole time, too. She's holding their six-year-old daughter, who's asleep on her shoulder. Dr. Bradley and Jack are mingling with other guests excitedly, and Jack keeps looking behind him at Caroline and grinning. She refuses to acknowledge him, but even from my hiding position I can see her legs shaking. I've never seen Caroline afraid. Never seen her anything more than totally confident, in control, powerful. But as she stands with her arms pinned behind her, voice shuttered, behind her captor and his family, she looks almost frail. It's like she's shrinking before my eyes.

"Waverly." Pari tugs on the hem of my skirt. "What's happening?"

I climb back down the ladder, the hum of the helicopter ringing in my ears. "Caroline is at the back with the Bradleys. She's got two guards on her but she's close enough to the main stairwell door to the roof that I think we could grab her."

"We can use this." Max pulls something out of her dress. A Taser. "I snatched it on the staircase. One of the guards dropped it. I knew having pockets sewn into this gown was a smart idea."

Pari and I both high-five her. "Yes, Max!"

"At least one of the guards with her has a Taser, too," I say.

"Mason and more of his guards are scattered around the rooftop. Once one of their guys goes down, they'll pounce. This isn't going to be a simple smash-and-grab. Unless . . ."

I scratch the back of my neck, running through different scenarios in my head. "If we can distract the guards, cause enough of a scene that the dudes holding Caroline will let her go for a second—"

"Then we could pull this off," Pari says. "We just need something to distract them."

I look around the balcony, as if a box with the word "distraction" is sitting somewhere just out of view, waiting for me.

Pari starts pacing back and forth. "Webber is the big boss, so the guards would have the fastest response to something that threatened him. Something Webber would want taken out."

"Or someone." I swallow hard. "Like me."

Pari stops and turns to face me. Max drops her gaze.

"It has to be me," I say. "All I've done tonight is cause trouble for him. He sent Ash across the ocean to keep her away from me. No one else gets under his skin like I do."

"He could take you," Pari says, her voice quiet. "Or worse."

I nod, but the pit in my stomach grows. "Maybe. But I have to do something. All this time, you've been trying to warn me about Webber, and I didn't listen. It was just easier for me to ignore the bad because I'd been promised so much of the good. I was wrong, and now it's time for me to do something right. I'm just sorry it's too late."

One of the helicopters' blades whir faster, and it starts to rise off of the roof with its precious cargo. Another one waits among the borealis clouds, ready to descend and take the last of Webber's highest rollers to the bunker.

It's now or never.

Max nods at me. "We'll take the stairs to the rooftop door, wait until the guards are distracted, then pull Caroline inside." Then, in a surprising move, Max pulls me into a hug. "Don't die."

Once she steps back and goes inside, Pari stares at me. "I'm not hugging you."

"Okay," I say.

"I'm not hugging you because you're gonna be fine." A tear falls onto her cheek and she wipes it away like it's an annoying mosquito. "I'll see you soon."

"See you soon."

Before I can overthink what I'm about to do, I turn away from her and start climbing the ladder again. Adrenaline pumps through me even though my stomach twists itself into a nauseated knot.

The first helicopter is just another light in the sky now, and the second is slowly coming in to land. The other rooftops are empty, the families already on their way to the bunker. Only Webber, Ash, Caroline, and the Bradleys are left now, along with Mason and three guards.

The helicopter lands with a thud that sends tremors through the concrete. I wait a few beats for Pari and Max to take their position at the door. It edges open an inch, Pari's face barely visible, but she gives me a thumbs-up, signaling me to make my move. Webber starts walking toward the helicopter, and

I launch into action, sprinting toward him. My hair blows wildly in the wind, but my gaze is fixed on him. He hasn't seen me yet, but Mason and the guards must have.

Webber doesn't hear me coming up behind him, and the second I'm close enough, I reach my arms out and tackle him to the rooftop. The skin of my wrists and elbows scrapes against the rough concrete, and the sleeve of Webber's suit rips on the landing. The pain in my shoulder sends shock waves throughout my body, but I push through it. I manage to get a couple of decent punches in, one cracking his nose and the other colliding with the side of his jaw, before strong hands grip my arms and pull me off of him.

"Don't hurt her!" Ash runs over, but Webber holds a hand out to stop her.

"Shut up, Ashley," he grunts. He climbs to his feet, his suit ruined and nose bloodied, and I can't help but feel proud of myself for messing him up a little bit. I steal a glance over my shoulder in time to see Caroline disappear through the rooftop door with Pari and Max. One guard is on the ground, flopping around. It makes me think of Frank and how he went down, but I brace against the image to stay in the moment, now. The other guard grips my arm so tight it hurts. Jack and his dad are too focused on me to notice Caroline is gone. Mrs. Bradley is already climbing into the helicopter, strapping her daughter into one of the dozens of seats.

We did it. Whatever happens now, we saved Caroline from being turned into Jack's Stepford Wife. And royally screwed up Webber's plans.

Webber undoes his crooked bow tie, glaring at me. "I really have to hand it to you, Waverly. You have fight in you. Nothing like your parents at all."

I bare my teeth at him. "Don't talk about my parents."

He laughs. "You know, I thought about inviting you to this year's masquerade. A legitimate invite, I mean. Back when I was personally going through the enrollment list, curating the Gateway, seeing your name gave me pause. You've always been loyal, a quiet follower, someone who could be a diligent foot soldier. But your influence on Ashley concerned me. You were too much of a distraction for her, so ultimately you didn't make the cut. But after seeing you fight me at every turn this evening, I'm beginning to think I made a mistake. You're a liar, a sneak, someone who will do whatever they need to in order to get what they want." He nods toward Ash, the girl I came here for tonight. "You and me, we aren't so different."

I want to puke. A part of me worries that he's right, but I shake that thought off. He's a killer, a liar, a man who has more power than most people will ever have and yet still wants more. That's not me. I won't let that be who I am. "I'm nothing like you."

"Did you or did you not," he starts, "lie about who you are to get into this party, just so you could stalk my daughter?"

Ash takes another step forward. "Don't listen to him, Waverly." I don't let myself look at her. I'm afraid of what I'll see in her eyes, and I can't be fooled again.

Webber ignores her. "You really have worked hard to screw up all my plans. You even managed to scare some of my people away." He tuts, then shakes his head. "I never knew you had it in you."

Neither did I, but I'd never give him the satisfaction of telling him so.

"But there was something you did know." I pull against the guards holding me, and their fingers squeeze my arms. "You knew about the solar flare."

He smirks. "I did."

"And now you and your phony generals are fleeing the city like cowards."

Webber scoffs, waves me off. "Don't be ridiculous. We're leaving the city like heroes. We're going to preserve the best of us. We all know what would happen if we stayed here. We've all heard them in the streets, chanting *eat the rich*. The masses would descend on us like vultures; they'd tear us to pieces for our resources. No, no, no. I've built something special, somewhere far away from the chaos. Somewhere we can all be protected."

"Did you build Cassandra, too?" I ask.

He laughs, then shakes his head. "You certainly know a lot about all this. Almost like somebody has been leaking information." Webber shoots a glare at Ash, who looks away. "Cassandra is a profoundly innovative predictive AI, the kind of which we had never seen before. My dear friend Gregory helped me build her. And now that he's abandoned us, Cassandra is completely under my control. She detailed for us the precise timing of tonight's solar flare. She gave us the key to the future and allowed us to gather all the resources, supplies, and allegiances we needed to start a new world. Cassandra is a masterpiece."

"So how long have you known?" I ask. "About the flare?"

He shrugs. "About a decade, give or take."

My jaw drops. "Ten years? You've been preparing for this for ten years, and you didn't think to warn the world about what was coming?"

"Oh," he says. "I thought about it. But what would be the point? The best scientists have been warning about climate change for fifty years, and the world did nothing. Why would this be any different?"

"Bullshit," I snap. "That's not why you kept it a secret. You didn't tell people because you wanted to hoard all the resources. You wanted total power, total choice over who lives through this and who doesn't."

Webber smirks, giving himself away. "And what's so terrible about that? Have you seen the state of the world lately? We need true leadership, someone to take control and bring the right kind of people together."

The right kind of people. Fucking monster.

"And you charged top dollar for front-row tickets to the apocalypse. Survival of the richest," I say.

Webber's brows pinch together, his eyes piercing right into mine. "Survival of the richest? No, no, no. Survival of the toughest. The smartest. The hardest-working. Without people like me, people like you would have nothing. We give you everything, and you still want more. But in the world I'm creating, everyone knows their place. We all have contributions to make to the Gateway, to the family. And we all get exactly what we earn, no more, no less."

"How exactly did you earn what you have?" I ask. "You were born into wealth and power that was built on the backs of immigrant women. Then you took that and turned it into a so-called school for old-money families, churning out more people just like you."

He raises an eyebrow, the corner of his mouth lifting into a smile. "If what I've built is so terrible, Waverly, why are you here?"

A lump forms in my throat. I don't have a smart-ass answer to throw back at him, and it's killing me. And I hate to admit it, but he isn't totally wrong. I wanted to be included in his world.

For so many different reasons. The system is broken, but it's the only way to play the game. Someone like me would never in a million years get into Yale premed and then the School of Medicine without the Webber Academy name on my scholarship application form. My parents see private education and the connections it brings as the only way for me to live a life more financially secure than theirs. But he knows all this. He knows how to play the game because he helps create the rules.

"Dad." Ash takes her father's hand. "Stop. You've won, okay? Leave her alone." I should be furious with her, but seeing her beg like this only makes me feel sorry for her, and hate him even more.

He shakes her off of him, and the way she shrinks at his rejection tears a hole in my chest. "Hmm?" he continues taunting me. "Why did you apply for and accept my generous scholarship? Why have you shown up at the academy every single day trying to claw your way up the ranks? Why do you try so hard to be one of us?"

Anger burns inside me. I spit in his face. He flinches, then reaches into the breast pocket of his tuxedo, pulls out a crisp white handkerchief, and wipes his cheek. Then, he calmly re-folds it and tucks it perfectly back in his pocket. In a split second, rage flashes in his eyes, and I know what's coming, but not soon enough to do anything about it.

He slaps me hard, the impact stinging my cheek so bad it makes my eyes water. But I hold my reaction in. I refuse to let him see me whimper. Instead, I hold my chin high, forcing myself to stare into his cold, dead eyes.

"Don't you touch her!" Ash pushes him once, twice, and on the third he snatches her wrists and holds her still.

"This is who you've been fighting so hard for all this time?" he snarls. "Some kid from Queens whose parents have spent their whole lives cleaning up after people like us just to be in our vicinity? Of all the choices you have, you choose her?"

Ash doesn't hesitate. "Yes. I choose her. I will always choose her."

What? She must be bluffing. Trying to make him mad. I'm just a pawn in her fight with her dad. But then she turns her gaze to me, and her expression softens, tears fill her eyes, and part of me believes her.

I have to force myself to look away, and it feels like I'm ripping the scab off a fresh wound. I don't know what to believe. This endless night has flipped my whole world upside down and inside out, I've lost faith in everything. So why am I still clinging so tightly to the hope that Ash really loves me, after all this?

My head spins like I've been hit with one of Mom's vertigo episodes. Ash is linked to everything I've seen tonight. She was in the cigar room when Jeff was murdered. But she screamed, she panicked, just like I did. Then the warnings she gave me in the Palms lounge, about her dad being dangerous. And then that kiss.

Oh, that kiss. It felt so real.

So did the way she held my hand in the Red Room. The tremble in her voice when she told me what really happened, that Webber had sent her away and controlled her every move.

Her fear seemed so real, I felt it in the goose bumps on my arms.

But then. She let Mason take me away after the Palms. And the code. Her fumbling fingers. Ash had to have input the wrong code on purpose, to get us caught. There's no other explanation. She betrayed us. She betrayed me. And this is just another attempt to screw with my head.

I can't let it get to me. I won't.

Webber's face turns dark, and he pushes Ash away from him with such force that she tumbles to the ground. It's like watching a porcelain doll shatter in slow motion, the way Ash seems to break into pieces so easily now.

"You're a fool," Webber snarls at her. He turns back to me, and this time he looks closer.

Then, in a low, sinister voice, just to me, he says, "And you're no good."

Something inside me ignites like the match I lit in the kitchen downstairs. Years of his lying and manipulation flash before my eyes. All the times my parents and I were looked down upon by people like him. The betrayal, how he made a big show of helping my mom while planning to leave us all to die. The lies. The greed. The destruction. It all comes rushing to the surface like a storm.

I let out a scream, pulling free from the guards' grip. My fists connect with Webber's jaw, his nose, his eyes. By the time Mason drags me off of him, Webber is bleeding even more and so shocked the color has drained from his face.

He stands up from the ground, patting at his tux to straighten out the creases. He swipes his knuckles under his nose and sees the blood. Then his eyes snap up at me in shock and anger. He takes a step toward me, but a loud boom stops him in his tracks.

"Let her go, Hulk!" Pari stands in the doorway, a sword pointed in Mason's direction. Max and Caroline stand behind her, holding Tasers.

Laughter erupts out of Webber. "Quite the crew you've assembled here. What a cute little rebellion. You even turned my own flesh and blood against me." He snaps his fingers and the remaining few guards attack the girls. Max gets the first one in the neck with the Taser, and he drops to the ground like a ton of bricks. I try to wrestle out of Mason's grip, but he twists my wrists tighter and pins my arms behind my back, laughing at me like I'm a fool for even trying to fight. Pain burns through my shoulder, and I feel blood spilling out and running down my back.

Pari runs toward us, a fierce fire in her eyes as she raises the sword with one hand. "This is for Frank!"

She swings the blade down, and Mason lets go of me to catch it in his hands, no doubt cutting his palms open. He manages to hold it there, trying to pull it from her grip, turning it into some kind of tug-of-war game. I jump up and hang off his back, my arms around his thick neck. I squeeze, feeling his Adam's apple rise and fall against my skin. A few feet away, Caroline and Max are standing back-to-back, Tasing anyone who gets too close.

"Owen!" Dr. Bradley yells from inside the helicopter. "Come on!"

"Mason," Webber barks. "Get Caroline. Forget about the rest of them. We just need Caroline!" Then he takes Ash by the arms and pulls her up. "Time to go."

Ash pulls out of his grip and backs away from him.

Mason lets out a growl and wrenches the sword from Pari; then, in a move straight out of WWE, he throws himself backward with me still clutching his neck. I let go, narrowly rolling out of the way before he slams into the concrete next to me. The sword flies like a missile, disappearing into the darkness over the edge of the building.

The force of my landing knocks the wind out of me, and my back seizes as I gasp for air. I feel like I'm suffocating, like the weight of this nightmare is finally crushing me beyond repair. My shoulder screams at me, my lungs burn, my eyes water. Pari kicks Mason in his ribs, and I worry she's going to injure herself. A guard pins Caroline to the ground, his hands around her neck, the Taser just out of her reach. Max wrestles for her Taser with another guard. I don't know how much more we can take. I don't even have the capacity to scream.

"Waverly." Ash kneels next to me, her balance slightly off. She holds her hand to her forehead, then shakes it off. "Are you—"

"Ashley, come." The dean beckons his daughter.

She runs a hand over my cheek. "No. I'm not going anywhere with you."

Behind her, Webber's eyebrows shoot up to his hairline.

Mason swings his legs and sweeps them under Pari, knocking her down. Then he stands up with a grunt and grabs me by the hair, pulling it so hard it feels like he's going to tear my scalp clean off. He does the same to Pari, and within moments we are both on our feet, his grip on us even tighter than before despite his bloodied hands. It's like he only gets stronger the more we fight him.

"Mason." Ash stands. "Let them go."

Webber takes Ash's wrist and spins her to face him. She moves her weight from one foot to the other, like she's struggling to find the ground underneath her.

"What exactly is *your* plan?" Webber demands. "Run off with Waverly to live with her parents in their roach-infested shoebox in Queens? Fight strangers for food scraps like subway rats and burn trash in the street to keep you warm when

winter hits?" He laughs, then shakes his head. "I've been preparing for this for a decade, child. I've built a new world for
you, to keep you safe and protected and give you a future. I
know you're mad at me, and the rebellious teen in you wants
to defy me, but you would never throw all that away for some
girl. You're smarter than that."

Ash slides her hand out of his. "I'm not going with you. I
should have stood up to you when you sent me to London, to
keep me away from Waverly. Well, I'm standing up to you now.
You don't care about me, you only care about having power
over me. It stops now. You can't control me anymore."

He takes a step forward; anger flashes in his eyes. "Clearly,
what I said about your mother earlier tonight was a mistake.
If she were here right now, if she saw the way you're behaving,
the disrespect and ungratefulness you are showing to your
own father—" The muscles in his jaw tighten. "Your mother
would be ashamed of you."

Tears fall onto her cheeks. She tries to slap him in the face,
but as she lifts her arm, she loses her balance. I try to break
free from Mason's grip to help her, but it's no use. Ash holds a
hand up to her forehead again, and her eyes suddenly seem to
roll back into her head.

"Oh . . ." she says, before falling.

Her dad catches her.

"Dad. You didn't."

My heart sinks. He drugged her, after all. Every ounce of
anger I had toward her melts away. She's just as much a pawn
in this game as I am.

CHAPTER TWENTY-THREE

Owen Webber strokes his daughter's hair as he looks down at her in his arms. "I had no choice, sweetheart. I knew you'd fight me. You are coming with me to the new world, whether you like it or not."

Ash tries to say something, but he covers her mouth with his hand.

"Shh," he says. "Don't try to fight it. You protest now, but one day, you'll thank me for this. I know you will."

The dean drugged her, just like he drugged everyone else. His own daughter. She screams as he and a guard drag her to the waiting helicopter. Mason holds me back, the noise of the helicopter blades drowning out my screams.

Ash wasn't trying to trap us in the security room. She wasn't fumbling with the key code on purpose. She was feeling the effects of the drugs. Guilt slices through me like a knife. How did I not see the signs? I turned on her so quickly. We all did.

Even after everything I've learned about Webber tonight, I still never thought he'd drug his own daughter. Clearly, giving a man like him the benefit of the doubt has been my downfall from the beginning.

I struggle against Mason, elbowing him in the sides, but I have a feeling it hurts me more than it does him. My shoe knocks something at my feet, and I glance down to see my mask staring up at me, its gold surface shimmering in the light from the rainbow sky. I slip the tip of my foot under it, then kick, flipping the mask up into the air. In a miracle, I catch it. Then I start wildly stabbing behind me, aiming for Mason's face, hoping one of the crown's rays will get him.

My arms twist and thrust the air a couple of times, making my bones ache. But on the third swing, I hit something fleshy and push the spike in as hard as I can.

Screams tear out of him, and Pari and I fall out of his grip. When I turn around to see the damage I've done, my stomach lurches. A spike from the mask is sticking out of his left eyeball.

He falls to his knees, cupping his face as blood spills out between his fingers.

"I'll help the girls," Pari says to me. "You get Ash!" She heads over to where Caroline and Max are struggling against the guards holding them, picking up a Taser on the way.

Before I can even turn around, someone grabs me around my waist from behind and throws me to the ground. I roll onto my back to see Jack lunging at me, his face battered from when Caroline whaled on him earlier, his hand wrapped up in a bloodied bandage.

"You're ruining everything!" he yells down at me.

His parents beg him to get back on the helicopter, but he ignores them. His hands reach around my throat, squeezing, his face contorting in pain from using his injured hand. I knee him in the balls, and he lets go, falling backward. Clutching my chest and trying to catch my breath, I climb to my feet, but he grabs my ankle, and suddenly I'm back on the rooftop, my head throbbing with pain from the hard fall. Next thing I know, he's on top of me again. We wrestle around, and then the ground gives way, and I'm sliding off the building. My fingers grip into the edge of the rooftop.

Jack laughs and leaves me there, dangling in the air, barely holding on, the strain on my stab wound bringing tears to my eyes. Smoke fills my nostrils, and I glance below to see black smoke seeping out of the factory. The fire I lit has spread into the bones of the building.

BOOM! Flames explode out of the first-floor windows, the heat and smoke overcoming all my senses.

Hold on, hold on.

I can't breathe.

Hold on.

I'm burning.

Hold on.

I'm losing my grip.

Just. Hold. On.

Someone takes hold of my hands. I blink through the smoke. Ash.

The flames stretch toward me like the claws of hell, trying to pull me into the inferno. If she lets go, that's it for me.

Ash grips my wrists, the only thing keeping me from falling to my death. My dress blows wildly in the searing wind. My shoes slip off and tumble the fourteen floors down, eaten by the fire.

"I've got you!" Ash yells down to me. Her words slur from the drugs.

She grits her teeth, then starts pulling me up. The skin of my forearms scratches against the gravel of the roof as I heave myself onto it. Once I'm safe, Ash pulls me into her arms and holds me. But we're still not out of the woods.

Mason stumbles to his feet, then scoops Caroline up and throws her over his shoulder. She screams as he runs to the helicopter, leaving a trail of blood behind him. The remaining guards see the smoke rising around us and give up their fight, racing to jump onto the chopper, too.

"Caroline!" I scream. Ash and I get up and run after her. Ash stumbles a few times, but she doesn't give up, despite the drugs in her system.

Caroline fights as hard as she can as Mason climbs into the helicopter. Her fists connect with Mason's chest, his shoulders, his face. Dr. and Mrs. Bradley grab Caroline by her wrists, pulling her inside like ravenous zombies. Ash and I each take one of Mason's legs, using our bodies to weigh him down. He's like a fucking cockroach that just won't give up. The helicopter lifts off of the roof, our chances of saving Caroline shrinking with every inch of air it gains.

Max and Pari join in, the four of us trying to save Caroline from being taken. Jack, another cockroach who just won't quit, starts kicking Ash's knuckles until she loses her grip on Mason's leg. She falls to the ground, and I see red.

I climb onto Mason's wide back, reach for Jack's collar. His eyes go wide.

"Dad!" he cries, but it's too late for his daddy to save him from me. I pull so hard I feel the cut in my shoulder rip open deeper. Jack somersaults through the air and lands ungracefully on his face. I make a mental note to laugh about it later, then get back to saving Caroline.

Mason crawls into the helicopter with me latched on to him. Webber is in the passenger's seat, screaming at the pilot to leave. But the smoke is so thick now that the windshield is covered, I can barely see two feet in front of me. The Bradleys are losing their shit because their boy is unconscious on the rooftop—we could jump out before they think to stop us.

"Jack!" his mother screams. "Wake up!"

Mr. Bradley pulls the headset off the pilot and tells him not to leave yet.

"Forget about it," Webber says to his friend. "We don't have time." Like Jack is a pair of gloves Bradley left in a cab and not his literal son.

"He's right!" the pilot yells. "The fire is compromising the building. We need to leave now."

They all start yelling at one another, Bradley throws a punch at Webber, and Mason lets go of me and Caroline to step in. I take Caroline's hand and we scurry to the edge of the helicopter, swinging our legs over. But just as we're about to jump, the helicopter lifts higher again, leaning to the left so hard we slide backward.

"Are you insane?!" Webber booms.

I pull myself toward the exit again, and Caroline does the same. When I peek over, we're way higher than just a second before. I swallow hard. This is gonna hurt like hell.

Through the smoke, I can see the shapes of Max, Ash, and Pari waving us down. And another shape standing up, too. Jack is alive, I guess.

There's another round of screaming from the grown-ups, and the helicopter swings again. We swoop back down so fast that my head spins. We don't land on the roof, but we're close enough that Jack jumps up and catches the edge of the opening. Shit.

"Dad!" he yells, but they're all too busy fighting to hear him.

"We gotta go," I say to Caroline. We take each other's hands, and jump.

I was right; it does hurt like hell. There's cursing. Silk all around me as I lie among the ball gowns of my friends. And then, my favorite voice whispering my name.

"Waverly," Ash says. She's on her side next to me, a fresh cut on her cheek dripping blood. But she's smiling.

Pari sits up and leans over me. "You good, bro?"

"I think so," I say. Everything hurts. But I'm alive. We made it out of the helicopter. When I look up again, Jack is climbing in as it lifts higher and higher. And thanks to the warring adults and thick smoke, they don't even seem to realize Caroline isn't there.

We stand on the edge of the Webber Sewing Factory rooftop, ready to descend the fire escape. I take one last look at the helicopter, knowing they can't come back for us—not with the building on fire like this. I see Webber standing in the open helicopter door, with Mason by his side. And then, in one violent movement, Webber pushes Mason out, his Hulk-ish body falling like a boulder into the water below.

Loyalty to Owen Webber only brings death and destruction.

I'm no fool; I know we haven't won. Not really. Webber will probably find a way into his billion-dollar bunker, even without Caroline. He and his cult of one-percenters will ride out this storm in luxury. But they'll turn on one another on a dime, too. I'd rather be out here in the chaos of it all with my true friends than in a safe house with people who are monsters behind their masks.

"Waverly?" Ash calls from two levels below. "You okay?"

I look down at her, and I still can't believe she's here. She's with me. Climbing down below her are Caroline, Pari, and Max. We're all here.

"I'm okay," I tell her.

Once we're all back on firm ground, we leave the Sewing Factory behind us to crumble. The Webber empire is falling. And when he comes back to this city, we won't let him or his allies reclaim it.

Beyond the city, the landscape is dark and unknown. Neon

clouds roll above us, and orange flames burn in every borough, but I'm not without hope.

Hope that I'll make it home to see my parents again. Hope that this determination, this fire I feel in my belly, will spur me on, fuel my fight. Pari takes Max's hand, and she takes Caroline's, and I take Ash's hand—and never plan to let go. We all link together like an unbreakable chain.

We may not have saved everyone, but we are alive to fight another day.

Tonight, we've proven that we are so much stronger than we ever believed.

We survived the end of the world. And when the sun rises, a new world will rise with it.

ACKNOWLEDGMENTS

From the time an idea sprouts in an author's head to the day it's held in a reader's hands, a book has gone through so many changes. It has been transformed by the care, insight, and talent of countless people, too many to name in just a short couple of pages, but I'll try.

First, to my agent, Lauren Spieller, for your tireless effort and enthusiasm—and for gently guiding me back to the task at hand when I inevitably let my imagination run off in a million different directions. Thank you.

To John Cusick and Mary Kole at Upswell Media, your endless encouragement, knowledge, and support got me through some of my worst bouts of imposter syndrome. Thank you for being on my team.

To Sylvan Creekmore, thank you for saying yes to Waverly's story and for being such a fierce champion for all queer stories. To Sarah Grill, you are brilliant. Your attention to detail and love of schedules were a salve for my anxious brain. To my iconic cover designer, Olga Grlic, and the team at Wednesday Books and St. Martin's Press, you are absolute rock stars. I couldn't have asked for a better team of people to work with on this book, and I feel incredibly fortunate. And to the sensitivity readers who so graciously shared their thoughts with me, I can't imagine how hard it is to do what you do, and I'm so thankful for your insight.

To all the booksellers, librarians, and teachers who have ever recommended one of my books, oh gosh, I'm just so grateful. I could gush about how much I love booksellers and librarians forever, but I have limited page space, so just know that I will fight to the death for you.

For all the readers, the Bookstagrammers and BookTokkers who have ever said kind things about one of my books, I can't even begin to thank you. Nothing makes my heart happier than to know someone saw themselves in one of my stories. Special thanks to Jupiter @bookstagramrepresent, Janai @janaireads-books, Janna @bookishjanna, Star @littlemissstar55, Nicoletta @nicolettawrites, Juliana @sherlockreads_, Sydney @sydneys.books, and Lucie @whatluciesreading, for supporting my work so much. I see you and I am grateful.

A lot has happened in my life between my last book and this one. My family and chosen family have been the glue that held me together more than once, even from the other side of the globe. To my parents; to Rob and Dale; to Camille, Pat, Chris, Nick, and Nana; to Mike; and to Christine and Amy: thank you for being there when it felt like the end of the world.

And finally, to my hot wife, MC, thanks for replying to my DM. Sorry the cats like me more than you.